Our Last
CRUSADE
OR THE RISE OF A
New World

"I haven't heard anything from her… What in the world happened to you, Rin?"

Aliceliese Lou Nebulis IX
Second-eldest princess of the Nebulis
Sovereignty. She is incredibly worried
when she loses contact with Rin and Iska,
who have gone to save Sisbell.

"You can't run now."

Nene Alkastone

Chief mechanic of Unit 907 of the Special Defense Third Division. She does everything in her power to stop Sisbell's love plot.

Mismis Klass

Commander of Unit 907 of the Special Defense Third Division. Also does everything in her power to put a stop to Sisbell's love plot.

Our Last Crusade or the Rise of a New World

"Y-you two?! But you were asleep!"

Sisbell Lou Nebulis IX
Youngest princess of the Nebulis Sovereignty. Aliceliese's little sister. She was abducted and taken to Kelvina but is saved by Iska and the others. She plans to strengthen her bond with Iska while Alice isn't around, but…

CONTENTS

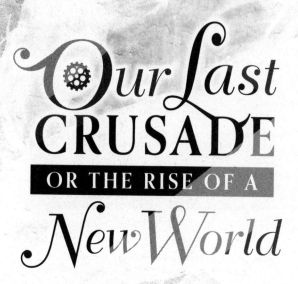

Our Last CRUSADE
OR THE RISE OF A
New World

10

KEI SAZANE

Illustration by
Ao Nekonabe

YEN ON

NEW YORK

Our Last CRUSADE
OR THE RISE OF A
New World

10 KEI SAZANE

Translation by Jan Cash
Cover art by Ao Nekonabe

KIMI TO BOKU NO SAIGO NO SENJO, ARUIWA SEKAI GA HAJIMARU SEISEN Vol.10
©Kei Sazane, Ao Nekonabe 2020
First published in Japan in 2020 by KADOKAWA CORPORATION, Tokyo.
English translation rights arranged with KADOKAWA CORPORATION, Tokyo, through
TUTTLE-MORI AGENCY, INC., Tokyo.

Yen On
150 West 30th Street, 19th Floor
New York, NY 10001

Visit us at yenpress.com
facebook.com/yenpress
twitter.com/yenpress
yenpress.tumblr.com
instagram.com/yenpress

First Yen On Edition: November 2022
Edited by Yen On Editorial: Shella Wu, Maya Deutsch
Designed by Yen Press Design: Liz Parlett

Yen On is an imprint of Yen Press, LLC.
The Yen On name and logo are trademarks of Yen Press, LLC.

The publisher is not responsible for websites (or their content) that are not owned by the publisher.

Cataloging in Publication data is on file with the Library of Congress.

ISBNs: 978-1-9753-4306-4 (paperback)
       978-1-9753-4307-1 (ebook)

10 9 8 7 6 5 4 3 2 1

LSC-C

Printed in the United States of America

Our Last CRUSADE

OR THE RISE OF A

New World

So Se lu, deus E gilim fert?
What tale do you weave?

Nevaliss E suo Ez nes pelnis, Ec wop kis Sec eme cs.
You call this a fleeting vessel, but even it is a gift I bequeathed to you.

Deris E nes Sec phenoria.
Because you are also my child.

Utopia Powered by Machines

THE HEAVENLY EMPIRE

Iska

Member of Unit 907—Special Defense for Humankind, Third Division. Used to be the youngest soldier who ever reached the highest rank in the military, the Saint Disciples. Stripped of his title for helping a witch break out of prison. Wields a black astral sword to intercept astral power and its white counterpart to reproduce the last attack obstructed by its pair. An honest swordsman fighting for peace.

Mismis Klass

The commander of Unit 907. Baby-faced and often mistaken for a child, but actually a legal adult. Klutzy but responsible. Trusts her subordinates. Became a witch after plunging into a vortex.

Jhin Syulargun

The sniper of Unit 907. Prides himself on his deadly aim. Can't seem to shake off Iska, since they trained under the same mentor. Cool and sarcastic, though he has a soft spot for his buddies.

Nene Alkastone

Chief mechanic of Unit 907. Weapon-making genius. Mastered operation of a satellite that releases armor-piercing shots from a high altitude. Thinks of Iska as her older brother. Wide-eyed and loveable.

Risya In Empire

Saint Disciple of the fifth seat. Genius-of-all-trades. A beautiful woman often seen in a suit and glasses with dark green frames. Likes Mismis, her former classmate.

Paradise of Witches

THE NEBULIS SOVEREIGNTY

Aliceliese Lou Nebulis IX

Second-born princess of Nebulis. Leading candidate for the next queen. Strongest astral mage, who attacks with ice. Feared by the Empire as the Ice Calamity Witch. Hates all the backstabbing happening in the Sovereignty. Enraptured by fair fights against Iska, an enemy swordsman she met on the battlefield.

Rin Vispose

Alice's attendant. An astral mage controlling earth. Maid uniform conceals weapons for assassination. Skilled at deadly espionage. Hard to read her expressions, but has an inferiority complex about her chest.

Sisbell Lou Nebulis IX

Youngest princess of Nebulis. Aliceliese's little sister. Possesses Illumination, which reproduces footage of past events. Saved by Iska when she was captured in the Empire.

Lord Mask On

A member of the House of Zoa, which directly competes with the princesses for the throne. A conspirator whose true motives are unclear.

Kissing Zoa Nebulis

A powerful astral mage. Called the favorite child of the Zoa. Possesses astral power of thorns.

Salinger

Strongest sorcerer. Imprisoned for attempting to assassinate the queen. Currently at large.

Elletear Lou Nebulis IX

Eldest princess of Nebulis. Focused on traveling abroad. Often absent from the palace.

PROLOGUE

Those Who Reach for the Heavens

"Hey, are you listening, earth witch? I know you can hear me."

Hee-hee-hee. She heard a sound like a child holding back a giggle. An androgynous voice echoed throughout the large room laid with tatami mats.

It was an exotic feature, as they were not commonly used as flooring in the Empire, yet the entire room was filled with them and choked with the smell of incense. To Rin, who had been so unceremoniously dubbed the "earth witch," the sight of the crimson room almost seemed as if it had come from another world.

"You there, witch," her captor said again.

"…" She was silent.

"Didn't hear me? How odd. I'm sure you must be awake by now. Or are you just pretending so you can get the better of me in my sleep?"

"…Tsk! You monster."

There was no use attempting to deceive her kidnapper. With her hands still bound, Rin got up from the ground onto her knees.

The reception area was as expansive as a gymnasium. Save

for her, no one else was in the room except one other being—a *beast* that spoke the human language. The fox-like being sat cross-legged on a throne and looked down upon her, head propped in their hand. The beast grinned.

"Well, I see you're in a jubilant mood. Is it because you managed to capture me?" Rin quipped.

"Hm? Well, whether I take any enjoyment from this depends on your next actions," the beast replied.

"What's that supposed to mean?"

"Well, before we get into that, witch—"

"Shut your mouth!"

Witch—the word had triggered Rin into shouting and baring her teeth. It was the derogatory word used for astral mages.

"I hardly think you're qualified to call me that, considering your repulsive form!"

"Now, that's a bit upsetting. Am I really that ugly to you?"

The beast's silver fur was like that of a fox, and their face was a cross between that of a cat and that of a human girl. Their eyes were as large as a kitten's, and nearly as friendly, too.

A beastperson. Rin was completely unaware that race existed in her world, and so she asked, "What the hell are you?"

"That question again? Come on, how many times are you going to make me answer that?" the fox-like beast said with a yawn, tired of being asked the same thing over and over. "I'm just Meln."

"...You mean the Lord, Yunmelngen?"

"Oh, so you *do* know who I am, then," the Lord responded.

"You think I'd actually just believe that?!"

The Lord was the very symbol of the Empire, and therefore Rin's sworn enemy. Then again, it wasn't quite right to describe

them as *only* Rin's enemy. They were hated by Alice, the lady Rin served; the queen; and all astral mages alike. But that aside...

She never would have guessed that this beast could be the Lord.

"You have no right to call me a witch when you're a monster!" she said next.

"Now that's a misunderstanding," Lord Yunmelngen countered.

"What?!"

"Well, you're the one who wouldn't tell me your name."

"Of course I wouldn't. I'd never give my name to someone like you."

"Then what else could I call you other than *witch*? Stubborn much?" The silver-haired beast shrugged, feigning resignation, then continued. "Seeing as you're my prisoner, I think you're in no position to refuse to tell me."

"..." Rin kept silent.

She remained kneeling, her eyes closed. That was Rin's response—*I won't listen to you.*

A captured mage had one of three fates: execution, interrogation, or human experimentation. Any was fine with her. She would rather meet one of those three unfortunate ends than follow the orders of the beast before her.

"Ahh... So obstinate," they said. "A fine specimen of the Sovereign people, you are. You start seeing red the moment you hear *anything* about the Empire or Imperials."

She heard the Lord sigh again.

"Well, what to do with you? In times like these, I'd normally rely on Risya to win you over. Unfortunately, she won't be back for a while."

"..."

"Oh, I know!"

The silver-haired beastperson snapped their fingers.

Before it could even register in her mind, Rin found she had been unshackled.

"Uh?! What did you...?"

She opened her eyes instinctively. Now that her hands were freed, Rin readied herself and glared at Lord Yunmelngen, who stood atop a platform.

"I have a brilliant idea," they proclaimed.

Then the beast leaped. Like a cat, they somersaulted through the air and landed right in front of Rin.

"So," the Lord began.

"Guh!"

Rin jumped back in a panic. The silver-furred beast peered at her face, just five yards away.

"Now, I can tell you don't like me."

"That goes without saying," Rin replied.

"But, you see," the Lord said, "I'm bored. So let's have a competition, shall we?"

"...A competition?"

"Come at me with all you've got, witch."

The beast's beautiful, fluffy tail swayed to and fro.

"This will be a diversion for me, but it'll be a matter of life or death for you. Win, and I'll give you a reward. I'll let you go free from the capital, no strings attached."

"What did you say...?"

She doubted her own ears. Who would free a prisoner unconditionally? Especially one they had gone through all the trouble of bringing here?

The beast was *looking down* on her. The only reason the Lord had offered her that unbelievably convenient proposition was that they didn't believe she *could* win.

"Why, you little—! To what lengths will you go to make a fool of me?!" she cried out.

"Do we have a deal?"

Lord Yunmelngen spread their hands.

It was a declaration of war. This had to be the Lord preparing for battle, something no one in Nebulis Sovereignty history—not even the former queens—had seen.

"If I win, then you'll tell me your name. And you'll also entertain me until Risya is back. What do you say?"

"You're underestimating me. You think that just because I'm an earth astral mage that I can't fight in a room without earth?"

She whipped up her skirt. A moment later, Rin held two combat knives in her hands.

"Oh? You still had weapons?"

"I'll make you regret ever uncuffing me!"

She leaped off the tatami mat.

The intense scent of rushes wafted throughout the reception hall as Rin charged straight toward the Lord.

CHAPTER 1

My Four Guards and I

1

Imperial territory. Easternmost Altoria jurisdiction.

A hotel room in a town on the eastern tip of the Empire.

"It's me. Can I come in?"

"Iska?" Nene answered from beyond the door. "Of course! I'll open up right away!"

Then Iska heard the sound of footsteps, and the door burst open in front of him.

"Morning, Iska!"

A girl with a voluminous red ponytail greeted him. Like Iska, Nene was part of Unit 907. She was in charge of its communications equipment.

"Hurry, come on in. The commander just got started on breakfast."

"And how is *she* doing?" Iska asked.

"Sleeping on the sofa. She hasn't managed to get up quite yet."

"I guess I should have expected that..."

He headed inside while they talked.

Morning rays filtered into the room. The first thing Iska noticed was the commander buttering freshly toasted bread.

"Good morning, Commander Mismis," he said to her.

"Oh, morning, Iska," she replied.

"Is Jhin still asleep?"

"He's been awake. He even went out for a run around the hotel. I just saw him get back and start taking a shower, so he'll probably be here any minute."

"Got it. Then we'll start the morning meeting once he gets in." Mismis nodded, biting down on the toast in her hand.

"Any appetite?" Iska asked.

"Me?" she asked. "Oh, same as usual. I think I could have two slices of toast for breakfast, easy-peasy."

"Oh...um. I meant *her*." Iska glanced at the girl splayed out on the sofa behind them. Her strawberry-blond hair glittered gold in the sunlight showering upon her. She looked as charming as a doll while she slept.

Sisbell Lou Nebulis IX.

She was a witch, the enemy of Imperial soldiers. For the time being, however, Unit 907 had promised to protect her until she was able to return to the Sovereignty.

"How is Sisbell doing?" Iska asked again.

"Oh, I guess she didn't have any dinner yesterday... Nene got a nutrition drink for her from the hotel restaurant, and she managed to get that down, at least."

"Does she have a fever?"

"It was about ninety-nine or a hundred degrees when we took it at dawn."

"That's higher than last night..."

Someone had placed an ice pack on Sisbell's forehead. The night before, she'd fainted and developed a fever. Sisbell refused to be seen by any Imperial doctor, so the group could only guess what could have caused the sudden bout of illness.

"I think it's from fatigue...," Mismis offered.

"I agree," Iska said. "She was tied down to that bed in the astral-power research facility the entire time, so that must have something to do with it. And she didn't have anything to eat."

Indeed, Sisbell had been taken prisoner because of the great astral power that dwelled inside of her—because she was a witch. After being kidnapped and taken to a mad scientist named Kelvina, Sisbell had been alarmingly close to becoming a subject of human experimentation.

"I want subjects who are purebred. Very difficult to find in the Empire, I'm afraid.

"I won't let you escape."

Kelvina had locked her away in a room thick with dust and mold. Sisbell must have been scared to death during that time, not to mention being hungry and immobile because her captor had tied her to a bed.

...Plus, the Empire is enemy territory to her. She was all alone while she was imprisoned.

...The anxiety must have taken a huge toll on her body and mind.

Actually…it was practically a miracle she'd fared this well after going through all that. Iska had feared the worst when Sisbell was spirited away by the Hydra's mercenaries, so he'd been surprised but grateful for the state they'd found her in.

"…Ngh." Sisbell shifted slightly in her sleep.

Her sweet eyes fluttered open ever so slowly as the present members of Unit 907 watched.

"…Good morning, Iska," she said after a long pause.

"Are you up to talk?"

"My head hurts. And…I see four of you, Iska. You're out of focus."

"Sounds like you're *really* dizzy, then."

"Yes. It's terrible."

A weak smile crept across Sisbell's face. Her eyes still looked red and puffy, an indication that her fever had yet to break. She faltered just speaking to him, almost as though she were out of breath.

"I feel horrible…but I'm already much more at ease than when I was Kelvina's prisoner. The research facility was abhorrent. She bound my arms and legs to the bed, and the smell of the mildew in the room made me cough."

"Right. The building was disguised to look abandoned, after all."

"It actually *was* abandoned. Spiders and centipedes crawled all over my arms, legs, and even my neck as I lay there unable to move. I was hoping for death to claim me."

"Blech…"

"And then there was the restroom situation, of course. Now,

if you'd like to know exactly how I managed when I was immobilized for three days—"

"Okay, that's enough." Iska lifted a hand and put an end to Sisbell's rant. "We know it was a harrowing experience. I'm sorry we took so long. So just sleep for now. You're using up your strength by talking."

"……You're right." A demure smile flitted across Sisbell's face as she covered herself in her terry cloth blanket. "But you don't need to worry about me. This is all part of my strategy."

"Your strategy?"

"Well, if I win everyone's sympathy right now, you'll all be nice to me, yes?"

"…"

"And I mean you as well, of course, Iska."

"…Well, fever or not, I'm glad you could muster enough strength to come up with a scheme like that."

Iska meant it. He was genuinely relieved she hadn't been mentally scarred from the terror of being kidnapped. Better for her to be overly talkative than mute from trauma.

…*She isn't even crying or complaining in the slightest.*

…*Sisbell really is Alice's sister.*

Though she looked delicate and almost ethereal, he could tell she was resilient, a quality befitting a Sovereign princess.

"But…" Sisbell hesitated. "Rin was captured because of me. And by the Lord, of all people."

Suddenly, the atmosphere in the room shifted. When Sisbell mentioned the Lord, Nene and Commander Mismis shot their eyes open.

*   *   *

"Third Princess Sisbell. Let us have a conversation in the Imperial capital. This also concerns you.

"I will be waiting, Successor of the Black Steel."

It had happened immediately after their battle with the malevolent angel Kelvina. Just as abruptly as he had arrived, Lord Yunmelngen had whisked Rin away as his hostage. That was what the beast had said to Iska and Sisbell at the time: *Let us have a conversation in the Imperial capital.*

Rin's life was on the line.

Though they could have made their way straight to the capital, Unit 907 was conflicted. The invitation hardly guaranteed it was safe for them to go. Regardless of the circumstances, protecting a witch princess was as good as betraying the Empire.

…We need to be prepared when we go to the capital.

…They might capture us along with Sisbell and send everyone to the gallows.

"Hey, boss. You here?" Jhin, a young man with silver hair, carried a black device as he made his way over to them. "You left your comm in our room."

"Uh, what?! Oh right, I was looking for that. I'd lost track of where I left it. I'm glad you found it."

"It started making this ridiculously loud noise earlier. I dunno who was trying to call, though."

Jhin tossed the communications device at her. Mismis caught it and stared at the screen.

"…Huh?"

Her eyes went wide. She blinked.

"What is it, boss?"

"I'm not sure who this is. There's no sender ID. It can't be from anyone I know or HQ, either. Nene, do you know who this could be?"

"All right, let me take a peek, Commander." Nene took the device from her hands. "They've purposefully set this up so the sender's details won't be displayed."

"Huh? You can do that? But this is standard Imperial equipment."

The caller had been obscured. An Imperial forces communications device shouldn't have needed that function. The comms were supposed to show the name of the caller, along with their affiliation and rank.

"Come on, boss. Hurry up and read the message," Jhin said.

"…R-right. I'm a little scared to, though." Commander Mismis started to operate the device.

"What?!" She couldn't hold back her scream. "W-wait a sec?! Everyone, look at this! Iska, Jhin, and you too, Nene!"

As Mismis clutched the device in her hands, the screen glitched. Iska's breath caught when he read the text displayed…

"I'm having fun with the earth witch, so please take your time."

It was just that single sentence.

Just as Commander Mismis had said, there was no identifying information about the sender. Now they finally understood why. It was because there was no need to state whom it was from.

"This is…" Nene gulped.

"Their Excellency, the Lord… It must be… And 'the earth witch' has to be Miss Rin…"

"P-please show me as well!" Sisbell leaped up from the sofa. She staggered and swayed as she walked toward Commander Mismis to see her comm.

"…Shameless," Sisbell said. "It's like they're reminding us they have Rin held prisoner."

"You seriously think so?"

"What?" Sisbell turned around. She faced Jhin, who had been behind her. "Wh-what do you mean…?"

"I took it literally. I'm pretty sure the Lord must've sent this. Which means we haven't got to worry since Rin's still guaranteed to be alive. If they were planning on executing her, the Lord would have told us to hurry up before they offed her, right?"

"I—I suppose…" Sisbell raised her brows as she thought it over. "I've never heard of anyone telling you to 'take your time' after they've abducted someone—not even in a book. But why would they tell us that…?"

"How should I know? I think the part about 'having fun' with her is disturbing as hell, though. What do you think, Iska?"

"…"

When Jhin pointed that out, Iska slowly exhaled. "I'm…really conflicted, but I think I agree with Jhin. It doesn't feel like the message was meant to disconcert us or make us go faster. If anything, they might even be doing it out of consideration for your well-being, Sisbell. Like, telling us to make our way over slowly."

"M-my well-being?!"

"I think it's only natural to assume based on the timing. Seems like an idiosyncratic way of thinking, though."

Sisbell couldn't travel because of her fever. Yet as luck would have it, the message arrived just as she was about to rush to the capital out of worry for Rin.

"...I struggle to even comprehend it." Sisbell let out a large sigh.

She sat down on the sofa she had just been sleeping on.

"The Empire would execute or imprison any witch they got their hands on. Even Kelvina was on the verge of making me her plaything. So why would the Lord worry about my health? They're leading the very country that oppresses mages!"

"We don't get it, either...," Iska said, shaking his head as the agitation started to show in Sisbell's voice. "We're just an Imperial unit in the end. Nobody's going to tell us secret intel about the Empire. We don't have that standing. That's why none of us expected the Lord to look like that."

A beastperson with foxlike fur. If the Lord wandered through the capital looking like that, the Imperial patrol would come running immediately and make a scene.

"The Lord is portrayed as a middle-aged man with a beard on TV. No one in the Empire would think that isn't them. Even when I was promoted to Saint Disciple, Their Excellency remained behind a giant bamboo screen the entire time, so I couldn't get a glimpse of them. I only heard their voice."

"Did they sound the same?"

"No, their voice was completely different. They sounded like a gruff man. But now that I think about it, they might have been using a voice changer."

Iska hadn't even known what the Lord looked like. There was no way he could guess what the real Lord was up to.

"Curiouser and curiouser... I cannot believe Imperial soldiers like you wouldn't know who the Lord is," Sisbell murmured.

"Well, we know what we have to do to find out who he is. Go to the Imperial capital," Jhin replied, despite knowing Sisbell had been talking to herself. "But what I want to know is: Who are *you*?"

"......Huh?"

"This is the perfect opportunity. Let's clear this up right now," Jhin continued matter-of-factly from where he was standing. "Who are you, really?"

"C-come again?" Sisbell's eyes went wide, and her eyelids fluttered.

Jhin looked down at the darling girl, unfazed. "Remember yesterday? Kelvina called you Princess Sisbell. Right in front of us."

"Huh?! Th-that was..."

"And the Lord did, too. They called you the Third Princess Sisbell. Am I wrong?"

"..."

The strawberry-blond girl went silent.

Sisbell had been billing herself as a *servant* of the royal family since they had first crossed paths with her in the independent state of Alsamira. But that had all been a lie. She could no longer hide the fact that she was a Nebulis Sovereign princess. Her identity had been exposed.

"......Uh."

Sisbell, the third princess of the Sovereignty, bit her lip. She had pretended to be someone she wasn't. Unit 907 had believed they were protecting an envoy when it turned out they had been guarding a princess the entire time. This was a monumental breach of their agreement.

"Iska! What should we do...?" Commander Mismis whispered. "...I never would have guessed things would end up like this."

"...Neither did I," Iska said.

Luckily, Nene and Jhin had been focusing only on Sisbell.

Iska nodded so faintly that neither of them noticed.

...The commander and I decided not to tell them who Sisbell is.

...Because revealing that would have only dragged them into this mess.

He hadn't told Nene and Jhin—because he'd been afraid of this very situation.

He and the commander would likely be subject to disciplinary action once that fact they'd been guarding a witch princess came to light. Jhin and Nene, on the other hand, could have gotten off with a lighter sentence by simply claiming ignorance to headquarters. For this reason, Iska and Mismis had decided it was better if the other two were none the wiser.

...It would have turned out better.

...Just until we could take Sisbell back. If only Jhin and Nene hadn't figured out who she was.

He could never have guessed that the Lord himself would inform them of the truth. Even Sisbell could not have imagined the situation would pan out the way it had in her wildest dreams.

"We chose to be your bodyguards. But guarding a *princess* is entirely different than protecting a servant of the Nebulis royal family. Guarding you has a different implication now." Jhin stared down at the silent Sisbell. "It wasn't fair to us, at the very least. Don't you agree?"

"......What if...it *were* true...?"

Sisbell clenched her fists over her lap. Her face was flushed from her fever. She stared up at Jhin with large, quivering eyes.

"...Then what would you like to do...? Keeping this from you was *my* mistake. So would you like to cease protecting me?"

"..."

"Are you going to...disparage me because I'm one of the *loathsome* witch princesses?!" Her voice came out in a strangled rasp and echoed throughout the living room. "Please tell me. What will you do with me now that you know I'm a witch?!"

"Okay, but really," Jhin said as he looked down at Sisbell, who was deathly serious. By contrast, Jhin looked almost exasperated, as if the whole thing had been a letdown. "Did you *really* think we hadn't figured out your identity?"

"..."

"It was obvious."

".........What?" Sisbell's mouth hung open. "Uh, um?"

"I don't know any servant who speaks as high-handedly as you do."

"And Shuvalts called you 'lady' even though he's older than you," Nene added. "I was just talking with Jhin about it. We were fine with feigning ignorance until after we finished guarding you. But then Their Excellency called you Princess Sisbell, so it would have been a lot stranger for us to pretend we hadn't noticed, right?"

"...I—I...," Sisbell stuttered. "I suppose when you put it like that..."

"So there you have it. Your identity was obvious from the start. We just weren't completely sure yet." Jhin wore a straight face and crossed his arms. "We weren't going to bring it up, but then the

Lord went and called you a princess, so we couldn't keep up the ruse anymore. It would've been weird to not question it."

"I—I see! In that case—"

Sisbell leaped off the sofa. Despite her fever, she stood up and placed her hand on her chest. She posèd in the same way her older sister Alice did while declaring something.

"We've come all the way here," Sisbell said. "Our hearts practically beat as one—no, in fact, I daresay we were brought together by fate! Because of that, I will tell you everything about who I am as proof of my trust in you. In fact, I—"

"No thanks," Jhin mercilessly replied.

"Excuse me?!" Sisbell cried at the top of her lungs. "What do you mean?! I am a Sovereign princess, you know!"

"Yeah, and you admitted it, so I'm already satisfied."

"What?! Wait, where are you going?!"

"Back to my room. C'mon, Iska." Jhin moved away from the wall. He turned his back to Sisbell and left as though proclaiming his indifference. "I'm not interested in my clients' private lives."

"At least give me the chance to say my real name!"

2

Paradise of Witches, Nebulis Sovereignty.

The palace towering over the central state was known as the Planetary Stronghold. In one area lay the princess's private chambers.

"…What in the world happened?"

Alice propped her chin up with a hand and stared at the small monitor in the other at her desk.

Aliceliese Lou Nebulis IX.

The second of the three sisters born to the queen, she was called the Ice Calamity Witch by the Empire. She was feared for being one of the strongest astral mages.

At that moment, her eyes were sunken in from deep concern. Her dark expression was accompanied by her heavy voice as she addressed the screen. She had never been more despondent, even when she'd been on the battlefield.

She received no reply.

Since when had the communications ceased? Since when had the messages stopped coming from the person who *should* have been answering her?

"What's going on, Rin? You told me you would contact me back right away!"

After hearing nothing but radio silence from her attendant, Alice had realized something was amiss the night before.

"We've determined where Lady Sisbell has been detained. It's a facility that's been concealed as a deserted building.

"We will be breaking into it."

The Third Princess Sisbell was none other than Alice's younger sister. And Rin, who had declared she would go rescue the girl, hadn't been in touch since. Alice had a bad feeling about this.

…Did they fail to save her? Rin couldn't have been captured. No, she wouldn't just be captured…

…She would be tortured, *too.*

"N-no! Iska was with Rin, though!"

The Imperial swordsman Iska was Alice's greatest rival. She

could brag about knowing him better than anyone. Mortal enemy or not, she could never imagine he would break a promise he'd made with her.

...Rin should have been with Iska the whole time.

...They couldn't have both failed to rescue Sisbell.

Alice found that difficult to believe. But unless she assumed that was the case, it couldn't explain Rin's abrupt silence.

What should she do? Would it be best for her to consult with the queen as soon as possible?

...No. I can't assume that Rin was unsuccessful!

...I can't panic. Even if I did report this to the queen, I still don't know the whole situation.

It was possible that Rin's communications device wasn't working.

She would wait for today. Alice told herself that just as the light on the comm turned on.

"Huh?! A call!" She clutched the comm with both her hands, pitching forward as she pressed it to her head. "Rin! It's you, right?!"

"..."

"Rin?"

"Oh, it connected. It has been far too long, dear sister."

"...What?"

Alice doubted her own ears. This wasn't Rin's voice she was hearing...

"W-wait a moment. Is that you, Sisbell?!"

"If you are wondering how I unlocked Rin's communication device, I used my Illumination astral power to see when Rin—"

"Never mind that! Uh, um..."

This was such an unexpected development, she was at a loss for words. Her imprisoned little sister was in possession of Rin's communications device? Though Alice couldn't wrap her head around it, she concluded that Rin and Iska *had* safely rescued Sisbell.

"Sisbell, I need to ask," Alice said. "Are you all right?"

"They freed me. I still feel sluggish after being tied down for days, but the medication for my fever is beginning kick in."

"............I see."

Alice felt relieved. She needed to inform the queen at once. This didn't just mean that the queen's daughter had been saved—Sisbell's safe return would change the Lou's entire situation.

...We'll be able to expose the Hydra's entire scheme.

...Even Talisman won't be able to talk his way out of this if we have Sisbell's Illumination astral power.

The Hydra family had attempted to assassinate the queen. There were few who knew of the plot, but Alice was among them. She had been trying to deal with the lack of evidence as best she could, but with Sisbell safe and sound, her sister would be able to use her power to recreate undeniable proof of the attempt on the queen's life.

"Anyway, I'm just glad you're safe, Sisbell. We need to retrieve you from the Empire this moment so you can return to the Sovereignty. We have a great many things for you to do!"

"Yes, about that."

"What is it?"

"I'm afraid I must be the bearer of both good and bad news for you today, Sister."

"...And what news is that?"

"Which would you like to hear first?"

She thought for a bit. A vassal had asked her a similar question, so Alice knew exactly how to respond at times like these: "Tell me the bad news first."

"I'll tell you the good news, then."

"Was there any point in asking me, then?!"

"The great news is that I was saved."

"…I already know that."

She was aware. Alice had suspected that was the case. That was why she'd wanted to hear about the other information first.

"What's the bad news now? That it'll take you a few days to get back from the Empire? I don't mind that."

"Rin was captured."

"……Huh?"

"By the Lord. As in the *greatest enemy of the Sovereignty*—that Lord."

"…………………"

Alice froze.

Now it wasn't just her ears she doubted. She was so convinced this was a dream that she pinched her cheek on reflex. It hurt. This—undeniably—*was* reality.

"Sisbell?! T-tell me everything, starting from the beginning—"

"But please worry not, dearest sister."

For whatever reason, her sister answered in a victorious and cheerful tone.

"For I will *go save Rin!"*

"How?!"

"I will do it with my merry band of four guards."

"That does not help to clarify the situation! And why would someone such as the Lord even—"

"Please inform the queen."

"How am I supposed to explain this?! Oh, wait!"

She heard a click. She stared at the device, from which communication had been cut off only on her sister's side.

"...I cannot *believe* her."

Alice held her head.

3

The Empire, middle of the night.

In the far eastern jurisdiction of Altoria, a certain town quietly slumbered. Most of the rooms in Iska and the others' hotel had gone dark for the night.

And in that darkness...

"...Hee-hee."

Sisbell got up from the sofa, quietly giggling to herself. The living room was pitch-black.

Careful not to wake Nene or Commander Mismis, who were sleeping farther back in the room, Sisbell crouched low to the ground as she inched away. She opened the door and headed down the hall.

"...It's flawless, if I do say so myself. My late-night love plot!"

She was heading to the room next door. Yes, to the one Iska was sleeping in. She clutched the key she had pilfered in the afternoon as she walked through the corridor.

Ka-chak. The door opened with a light click. Her plan was as good as done now that she'd made it this far. All she needed to do was sneak into the room Iska was sleeping in.

...I was groaning about my fever into the afternoon.

...But in an unexpected twist, I'll use the deep of night to get even closer to Iska!

She needed a bodyguard.

They were heading to the Imperial capital now, and she knew not what would await them except that *Lord Yunmelngen* would be part of it. Because of that...what she wanted—no, *required*—was to be even more *emotionally* close to her guard.

"That means we must strengthen our bond, Iska!"

And so, she had hatched a plan that went like this... Step 1: Sneak into Iska's bed, claiming she still felt unwell. Step 2: Inch closer to Iska, claiming she couldn't sleep from anxiety.

She'd get just close enough to feel the heat of his body next to hers and vice versa. They would awkwardly settle in until they'd eventually fall into a peaceful slumber.

"The fact that I, the Third Princess Sisbell, am allowing a member of the opposite sex to be so close to me will be certain proof of my trust in him. You'll see, Iska!"

She had even dressed appropriately for the occasion. If she were to pretend to be half-asleep and wrap her arms around him, then the thin nightgown she had chosen to wear would allow him to feel her warmth through the fabric—or so she imagined.

There was a chance he would even be able to feel her heartbeat.

...Can you hear it, Iska? The flutter of my heart?

...Wait, that might be going too far.

Everyone knew Sisbell was something of a bibliophile, and even she would readily admit it. She was well aware from the romance novels she'd read that a girl of her age stopping by to meet someone of the opposite gender would invite misunderstandings. She, of course, would not be telling the queen of her actions. She didn't even want the queen to be aware this was happening.

"But it's not like that, Mother. I'm not doing anything questionable."

This wasn't a matter between a man and a woman, though she was also prepared in case it *did* come to that. She knew it was possible.

…Iska is at a certain age.

…But he's not the type who would force me into anything.

Sisbell felt comfortable approaching him to the point of sneaking into his room even in the dead of night. She simply wanted to feel comforted and safe. She wanted to be closer to him, and to see him blush. That was enough for her. She didn't intend to overstep more than that.

"…"

Still in the hallway of the hotel room, she stopped to consider things for a moment. Now that she thought about it, Iska wasn't the only one present. The sniper, Jhin, was here, too. He was likely sound asleep right now, just like Iska.

"This is perfect."

A mischievous grin spread over her face. Her heart pounded slightly in her chest as she took another step down the dark hallway.

"I'm going to be sneaking into Iska's room anyway. I'll pay a visit to that charmless boy, too, just to see what he looks like in his sleep. Regardless of how apathetic he looked in the afternoon, I'm sure he must be somewhat endearing while asleep. Ha-ha. I'll enjoy taking peek at a young man in the bloom of his youth… Eep!"

She tripped. Sisbell's foot had caught on something as she

tiptoed in, and she crashed loudly to the floor. Just when Iska and Jhin were so close at hand.

What had she tripped on?

As Sisbell rubbed her eyes, she spotted the glint of a thin thread.

"What?!" She couldn't help but shout. "A steel wire?! Wh-why is there a wire along the ground?!"

"Hee-hee-hee."

"Yeek?!"

She realized someone was behind her, but it was too late. They grabbed her by the shoulders, which elicited another yelp from her.

"There's no way?!" Sisbell said.

"...I knew it. I thought this might be what you were up to."

"Commander, aren't you grateful we set up a trap in front of Iska and Jhin's rooms?"

"Y-you two?! But you were asleep!"

Sisbell had no idea when they had arrived. Nene and Commander Mismis, who should have been fast asleep in the room next door, were standing behind her. They were both wearing cute pajamas as well...but the bold smiles on their faces were so frightening that Sisbell froze in terror.

"Hee-hee-hee. So, Miss Sisbell, where were you headed off to? Did you realize you're right in front of Iska and Jhin's rooms?"

Even in the darkness, Sisbell could still see Nene's eyes shine. For whatever reason, the red-haired girl held a rope in her hands.

"You stole the room key from my bag this afternoon, didn't you?" Mismis closed in on her—the commander held a pair of handcuffs.

"You can't run now."

27

"How about we make our way back to our room and have a *liiittle* talk. I think this feisty kitty needs a little lecture on common sense."

"W-wait! I... It's not like that!" She frantically flailed her hands at the two as they closed in on her. "I—I simply...j-just wanted to cuddle a little. I wasn't planning on doing anything unscrupulous—"

"Time for your punishment."

"Now let's head back, Miss Sisbell."

"Noooo! I—I was so close to reaching the garden of dreams...!"

She had only been two yards from their rooms.

With her goal just out of reach, Sisbell was bound and cuffed, then dragged back to the next room over.

4

The next morning.

"...Haah."

"Hm? You all right, Sisbell? You still don't look so great."

Sisbell, looking ghastly, had made her way to Iska, who was standing in the lobby. Somehow, she seemed even more haggard than the night before.

"...It was a terrible ordeal," she answered him.

"What was?"

"...I never would have fathomed they would lecture me into the night. No one's ever given me such a long scolding before, not even Mother."

"Um?"

"…Oh, it's nothing," she said.

She collapsed onto a lobby chair. As far as Iska could tell, she was steadier on her feet than yesterday in spite of her pale complexion. She wasn't nearly as flushed, either, so the medicine must have brought down her fever.

"Just to be sure, are you okay to travel today?"

"Why, of course." Sisbell lifted her face, looking livelier than Iska had expected, though she slumped into the chair. "The Lord asked for me specifically. If I tarry too long here, why, they might assume I'm frightened. How would that make the Sovereignty look?"

"Oh, there you are, Iska!"

"Sorry for the delay!"

Nene and Commander Mismis came out of the elevator. Jhin followed after them with the luggage.

"Boss, where are the train tickets to the capital?"

"Oh, I haven't reserved those yet. I was thinking of buying them at the station."

"Then we've gotta hurry. There aren't a lot of limited-express trains leaving from the boonies to the capital. If we miss this train, we might have to wait hours for the next one." Jhin started walking toward the hotel exit with their luggage in hand. "Well, I guess it shouldn't be hard to get five tickets, though."

"Wait right there. Make that *six*."

The exit opened. One glance at the person waiting there, and everyone stopped in their tracks, including Jhin, who was leading them.

"Risya…?"

"Hello there, Isk. And Mismis and Nene, too."

The woman cheerfully smiling and waving at them was none other than Risya In Empire, a Saint Disciple and the Lord's staff officer.

"Hey there, Princess."

"You!" Sisbell took a step back in surprise.

Risya had helped the Lord kidnap Rin. Sisbell must have found her despicable.

"What is the meaning of this?! You took Rin with the Lord and—"

"Oh, please stop right there, Princess Sisbell." Risya placed a finger against her lips, shushing the girl. "This is Imperial territory. And take a look, there are guards even in the hotel lobby. Don't you think it's in your best interest *not* to cause a scene, seeing that you're from the Sovereignty?"

"...Guh!"

"Well, I'm not here to talk about anything unpleasant. So, Mismis."

When Risya called her name out without any warning, the commander quickly lifted her puzzled face.

"Wh-what's going on, Risya?!" Mismis asked. "Weren't you supposed to wait for us at the capital...?"

"I'm here to accompany you."

Risya grinned and took off her glasses. She swung them around her finger at the hinge as she looked at each member of Unit 907, then finally at Sisbell.

"Special orders, direct from Their Excellency. They want me to escort all of you personally," the fifth seat of the Saint Disciples declared.

INTERMISSION

Rin's Great Miscalculation

The Lord's offices.

A four-story tower stood in dignified silence deep in the capital. On the uppermost floor, in a room filled with the smell of rushes…

"What's wrong, little witch? You're looking quite pale."

"…Guh…!"

Lord Yunmelngen quietly laughed.

Rin had no strength to muster a retort as she knelt, her shoulders heaving up and down.

"How…did…"

She bit her lip. An unending stream of sweat was dripping down her brow and chin.

"I…can't believe you're this strong…!"

"You've really let me down, witch." The beastperson's voice was cold as they swayed their silver tail to and fro. Then the Lord sighed. With disappointment and contempt on their face, they brought down their hand. "I don't see a point to even pitying you. I'll put you out of your misery."

"Huh! W-wait!"

"There, checkmate."

"Ahhhhhh!" Rin fell over and hid her face.

Before her was a shogi board.

"Looks like it's game over." The Lord quickly turned over Rin's king piece with their sharp claws. "There, I've won. How many was that again? Seventeen in a row? I wish the matches would last longer."

"Guh! I've still got more in me!"

Rin jumped back up. She grabbed the game pieces from the board and started setting up a new game without regard for the Lord.

"Again! One more time!"

"Oh? You've got guts—more than I gave you credit for. But there's an overwhelming difference in our abilities. You won't win against me without a strategy."

"Take that back! I'll make you cry this time… Wait, what am I doing?!" Rin stomped her foot loudly against the tatami mats. "I got caught in the moment. What is going on here?!"

"Hm?"

"What happened to our match? Weren't we going to have one?!"

Rin pointed at her own knives, which had been cast aside on the ground. Though she had unsheathed them just hours earlier, in the end, she hadn't gotten a chance to use a single one.

"You told me to come at you with all I've got! And said it would be a matter of life and death for me. And that you'd unconditionally free me and allow me to leave the capital if I won!"

"Well, obviously I meant if you won against me at this game."

"You're so misleading!"

"What? You couldn't possibly think I meant something as violent as that." The silver-furred beastperson picked up a knife. They scrutinized the Sovereignty-made blade. "Unfortunately, all of my guards are out today. I can't fight you right now."

"..."

That statement... Rin narrowed her eyes. "By *guards*, do you mean the Saint Disciples?"

"That's right. They were injured during the Sovereignty raid."

"Huh!" Rin leaped violently off the ground, hard enough to break the tatami mat. She charged right at Lord Yunmelngen, then thrust the point of a newly drawn knife at their neck. "Looks like you've got *some* self-awareness, then... That's right, you're the one responsible for sending the Imperial forces to attack our nation! How many of our kindred do you think were wounded in that attack? Even our queen wasn't spared!"

"..."

"What? If you have anything to say, spit it out now!"

"That wasn't my idea."

"What?!"

The tip of the knife quivered.

"Stop playing dumb! Who else could have ordered the Saint Disciples?!"

"The Eight Great Apostles."

"Huh?"

"Well, I guess that didn't clarify anything for you, at least." The Lord yawned leisurely, without a care for the knife at their throat. "The Eight Great Apostles don't show themselves publicly. It's no surprise the Sovereignty wouldn't know who they are."

"What are you going on about?"

33

"You'll understand soon enough."

The Lord flopped over onto the tatami mats. There were so many ways she could kill them. But the Lord showed so little hostility that Rin was taken aback despite being the one holding them at knifepoint.

"That was part of the reason we took you captive. The Third Princess Sisbell should be making her way here soon. We should be able to explain everything using her powers."

"Huh? ...What do you mean by that?"

Rin knit her brows. She had noticed a minute difference just then. For an instant, the carefree and friendly Lord had shown a fleeting hint of coldness in their tone.

Something like rage...

"There's something I'd like to know." The beastperson, still stretched out, placed a hand on their face. "It happened a hundred years ago. I want to know exactly who turned me into this."

CHAPTER 2

Cracks in Paradise

1

The Solar Spire.

The palace of the Hydra, one of the three Nebulis royal bloodlines. Topmost floor.

On the balcony, which boasted a sweeping aerial view of the nightscape, stood a handsome man and a beautiful woman, their bodies illuminated by a brilliant light.

"Good evening. I'm sorry for being late, Uncle."

"You're right on time, Mizy. Quite unusual of you to suggest dinner together."

The balcony had been arranged for them to share a meal.

Two sets of tableware had been placed on the pure-white tablecloth.

"Perfect timing, since I had something that I wanted to consult you about as well."

A muscular, middle-aged man greeted the girl with a smile.

He was Talisman, the head of the Hydra. He had deep-set eyes and a chiseled nose, and his beautifully gelled hair was a dull silver. He was a picturesque image of a man in his forties. His iconic white suit was so perfectly tailored that he almost seemed like a movie star on-screen.

"First, please sit."

"Well…if I may."

She grinned. The young girl, who was rather mature, sat across from Talisman.

Mizerhyby Hydra Nebulis IX.

The girl's hair was a shocking lapis lazuli blue. Talisman's niece, a princess promised the position of next head of the House of Hydra, was also a queen candidate.

"So, Mizy, how about an aperitif?"

"I'm sorry, Uncle. I'm still only seventeen."

"Oh, pardon me. I suppose you are."

When Mizerhyby pointed that out, quite charmingly, Talisman responded with a grin.

"Then I shall have sparkling apple juice prepared for you. La Khalte, Marchen, Alsbnyu, please take three of the most fragrant and high-quality apple varieties and create a blend, will you? Try to make sure it smells as if it weren't nonalcoholic."

Talisman snapped his fingers. He watched as the stewards behind him left the balcony.

"Now then, dearest Uncle, I have something unfortunate to report to you. I would like to tell you before we enjoy our meal."

"Is it about dear Sisbell?"

"Oh, did you already know?" Mizerhyby blinked in surprise at the head of house's quick reply.

"I thought I would beat you to the punch for once," she said.

"I didn't receive a report, of course. It's been twelve hours since I last received correspondence from the people I left Sisbell with. I can only take that to mean something has happened."

The Third Princess Sisbell had been rescued. They'd never expected it to happen just days after they'd gone to the trouble of shipping her out of the Sovereignty to an Imperial research facility for safekeeping.

"The Hydra are as good as finished if Sisbell returns to the Sovereignty. I will be executed, and you and the servants will be sentenced to life imprisonment."

"...I'm very sorry." Mizerhyby's shoulders trembled. Her round and charming eyes showed a hint of anger she couldn't hold back. "If I had simply kept the Gregorian Descant from being stolen..."

"I'd like Sisbell to take her time in the Empire, if possible. I believe we can manage to prevent her return to the Sovereignty, at the very least."

The Hydra family had tried to assassinate the queen. As long as they prevented Her Majesty from finding decisive evidence linking them to the attempt, the Hydra's lead in the conclave would be unshakable.

"The Lou will have a difficult time winning in the conclave without the centralizing power of their queen. And the Zoa's head of house, Growley, has been captured by the Empire as well."

The Lou and the Zoa had fallen.

The sun—the Hydra—was set to rise in the Sovereignty.

"I'd like to keep Sisbell tied up in the Empire until the conclave has concluded. Mizy, if you are able to become queen, we can hush everything up afterward."

"Yes, dearest Uncle. But how will we keep watch over Sisbell while she's in the Empire?"

"We shall leave that to the Eight Great Apostles."

"……"

Mizerhyby narrowed her eyes. The name Talisman had uttered was closely guarded as one of the greatest secrets within the Hydra family. Their coconspirators. In the Sovereignty, human experimentation on mages had been forbidden on ethical grounds, but that was not the case in the Empire. And since the Hydra covered the witch transformation research the Eight Great Apostles pursued in secret, the two factions had joined forces.

"Sisbell was able to escape thanks to Kelvina's blunder. Kelvina's superiors must atone for her mistakes. We need to ensure the Eight Great Apostles show up to the task."

The aperitifs were brought in. A sparkling wine for Talisman. He watched the bubbles rise in the glass.

"They are keeping Elletear under observation. So they simply will need to add Sisbell to their roster."

"May I have a word, sir?"

She had appeared without warning. The witch Vichyssoise, with her red hair and large earrings, stood in front of the balcony's railing.

The girl had successfully undergone the witch transformation process the Eight Great Apostles had been researching, losing her humanity in Kelvina's procedure.

"Ah, so it's you, Vichyssoise. Thank you for your patrol." The head of the household held his wineglass aloft to her. "Would you like something to drink as well?"

"...Sure. I'll have water. My body would reject anything else," Vichyssoise answered, quite serious. She leaned back on the railing. "Sir."

"What is it?"

"You can take this as a joke if you will, but what you said earlier... Please consider what will happen if you lose control. This may eventually get out of hand."

"I suppose you mean the Eight Great Apostles?"

"No."

"Then Sisbell?"

"...I mean Princess Elletear of the Lou."

When the witch answered, countless emotions showed on the head of house's face. Irritation. Fear. Rage. Bewilderment.

And, in addition to those, envy.

"I haven't been able to drink anything but water for a month. Even being in this human form has become increasingly difficult. I know I'm no longer human... So there's something that I can pick up on because of my current state."

"Oh?"

"She's beyond inhuman."

"You mean dear Elletear?"

"Kelvina administered 0.0002 percent concentration of that substance to me. That was enough to turn me into a witch. But she asked for 51 percent."

"Mm-hmm."

"Do you understand, sir? More than half of her has been

consumed with that substance. And she's still able to retain her sense of self. She's a monster."

The First Princess Elletear had been ridiculed by the retainers for being the weakest purebred in history and had left the Sovereignty of her own accord. Then she'd made contact with the Eight Great Apostles and volunteered herself for banned human experimentation.

And the result had been deemed a "failure."

However...

She was only called that because Kelvina and Eight Great Apostles had lost control of her.

"I was convinced I would be dealt with; Chief Kelvina would collect my astral body data and scratch her head day after day, after all. She claimed my compatibility ratio was too high."

"...So, then." Vichyssoise narrowed her eyes. "I think we should deal with her soon. She's no longer useful to the Hydra, right?"

The Hydra and Elletear had joined forces because their goal was the same—to capture Sisbell. Elletear had told the Hydra of her sister's location, so they had cooperated with her in kidnapping Sisbell. That plan was now over.

"She's a Lou at heart. I'm sure she doesn't think much of the Hydra and that she'll eventually betray us. I think we should uproot her before she's able to sow seeds of anything more we could do without."

"I'm grateful for your advice, Vichyssoise."

Talisman nodded, a calm smile gracing his lips.

"You ought to know that I've already told the Eight Great

Apostles of my intentions of doing just that. I have told them to keep her under perpetual observation and to get rid of her if they cannot control her."

"Oh, so you've already made plans, then."

"The same goes for Sisbell. She has her uses, so I'd like to keep her if we can, but it's a different matter if she fights back. What say you, Mizy?"

"I have no qualms whatsoever with the plan." Mizerhyby smiled. She brought the glass of apple juice to her beguiling lips. "The three Lou sisters are nothing but an obstacle in the conclave, as far as I'm concerned. But......"

"You have more to say, it seems?"

"Alice will be trouble. We do not know how she will retaliate once she's aware the Hydra have laid hands on her sisters. And it seems that she's out playing as the queen's proxy because of her mother's injury. She is only cooperating with us in public—"

She stopped right there. Mizerhyby pursed her lips, and Talisman raised his eyebrows just slightly. Then Vichyssoise disappeared.

The ring of a diminutive bell signaling the arrival of a guest echoed throughout the quiet balcony.

"My Lord." A young man in a black suit bowed. "You have a guest. What shall it be?"

"Please ask them to leave. I have no interest in anyone who would disrupt a meal I am enjoying without an appointment...but, just in case...please tell me the name of our boorish visitor."

"It is Lord Mask."

"..." A faint sigh escaped Talisman. "What could he possibly be scheming? Oh, the adviser of the Zoa."

*   *   *

The underground area was even bluer than the sky.

The Nebulis Palace. Isolated block.

The wide corridor built from a natural limestone cave echoed with the sound of dripping water.

"I apologize for bringing you all the way here, Lord Talisman."

The sonorous voice of a man in a metal mask reverberated throughout the cavern with an underground blue lake. "It is dinnertime, after all. I thought we could finish this with a simple report. I did not think you would join me all this way."

"It was no hindrance at all."

Clack.

Their footsteps resounded as they crossed the bridge over the water's surface. Princess Mizerhyby followed behind as Talisman took the lead in front of the adviser of Zoa.

"It has been too long, Lord Mask."

"Why, hello there, Mizerhyby. So even you are joining us, then?"

"Oh, there's no need to be so formal. Please, call me Mizy."

Mizerhyby bowed and brushed aside her blue bangs.

Ahead of where she looked…

…was an enormous glass casket.

A girl of thirteen, perhaps fourteen, slumbered peacefully beneath the glass. She had sun-bronzed skin and wavy pearlescent hair. Her sleeping face still looked young and charming.

"The Revered Founder…"

Mizerhyby's eyes narrowed.

The coffin had cracked. Though it had been designed so it

could not be unsealed unless a padlock bearing the queen's emblem was opened, the casket was close to breaking.

"As you can see, my Hydra family members," Lord Mask said, a delighted smile he could not hide gracing his face, "the Revered Founder is attempting to awaken."

"Are you sure someone isn't attempting to awaken her?"

"How outrageous, Lord Talisman. Yes, I will admit the Zoa family did in fact suggest that during the family conference, but this is the Revered Founder's own wish."

He was the Zoa's representative, and Talisman was the Hydra's head of house. They both towered at nearly six feet tall. Though the glass coffin separated them, their powerful presences were evident when they faced each other.

"What do you say, Lord Talisman? If we rouse the Revered Founder, we will have no reason to fear a full-scale war against the Empire. It will only be a matter of time before we are able to recover Growley from the Imperial forces."

"…"

"Ah, and there is one other matter. I nearly forgot something important."

Lord Mask theatrically clapped his hands. Anyone watching would have seen it as a cheap act. And it showed through in his tone and demeanor.

"The Empire has captured Growley, the head of house Zoa. But if you were to view it another way, he has likely seen the face of our traitor. The face of the traitor who has ties to the Imperial forces."

"Oh?"

"The Revered Founder shall awaken. Once she has, we will be able to launch a full-on attack on the Empire. If we do that, we will be able to recapture the prisoners of war from the Imperials one after another. In all likelihood, that will allow us to capture the traitor."

"I see. That is good news."

Talisman looked at the princess next to him.

"The Hydra wish for the same. Though there is no guarantee things will go according to plan. Still, I am thankful for the news that the Revered Founder is close to waking."

"I believe it is time to be on the defensive—whoever it was that made a deal with the Imperial forces should be, that is."

"..."

"The Revered Founder will awaken any day now. And soon the traitors will have more sleepless nights shivering in fear."

"Indeed. Well then, I shall be taking my leave." Talisman nodded slightly at Mizerhyby and turned, his back to Lord Mask.

"Excuse us, Lord Mask. I wish you a good night."

"Yes, and you as well, Mizy. And Lord Talisman. I wish you a good night." The representative of the Zoa nodded and grinned. He watched as they disappeared.

"I'm sure you know. The Hydra will eventually sink. The sun cannot shine in the night."

His stifled murmur echoed across the blue underground lake.

2

Morning, seven o'clock.

In the center of the Altoria jurisdiction in the eastern reaches of the Empire, there was a terminal station frequented by the odd tourist or businessman. The jurisdiction was so remote that it would take even a limited-express train nearly a day to journey from there to the capital.

"…We should be back home by tomorrow." Jhin sighed as he sat down on a bench. "Feels weird. We've been gone for so long, it's almost nostalgic."

"I feel that way, too," Nene said. "It's been a whole month since we left the capital."

Nene, who sat next to him, spoke in a slightly conflicted tone. Now that they thought about it, they had been gone a while. It had all started with the headquarters giving them an order.

"Unit 907, you have been ordered to go on special leave for sixty days."

"It would be best if you went somewhere far away. How would you feel about resting in an ally nation on the outskirts of the Empire?"

They had first headed to the independent state of Alsamira.

There, they had encountered Sisbell and were forced to enter the Sovereignty when she asked them to be her bodyguards. Now, after they had been pulled into their fair share of trouble and fighting for their lives…the Imperial capital was finally within sight.

"…Don't see anything that matches the incident," Jhin said.

"Huh? What are you reading, Jhin Big Bro?"

"The morning paper. I got it at the place where you bought the bread for breakfast."

Nene glanced at the newspaper Jhin had been reading. She perused the domestic news.

"You mean about the research facility where Miss Sisbell was kept captive?"

"Yeah. Even though it was supposedly abandoned, I bet at least a few hundred people saw the massive amount of astral energy that blew into the air—Iska."

He rolled up the paper and threw it toward the swordsman. Iska caught it and glanced through the news as well, but he didn't find anything relating to the facility where Sisbell had been held prisoner.

…There isn't even a mention of the place being an illegal astral power research institute.

…An intense astral energy surged into the air outside when we fought Kelvina, no questions about it.

Yet no one had noticed? No, there *had* to have been witnesses. And they would have reported that back to the Imperial forces.

"Risya."

"Hm? What's up, Isk?"

The Saint Disciple of the fifth seat turned around. He knew she must have been listening to their conversation up until now. Her reaction was an act, plain and simple.

"So HQ is still hiding what happened then?"

"Oh, you mean the events from yesterday? They'll make a formal announcement, of course. But not until after an official investigation is finished." Risya shrugged as though there weren't anything else to it. "I know you still find things suspicious, but the Imperial headquarters weren't involved with that research facility at all. The Imperial forces weren't, either. That's why they need to do a thorough inspection into everything, along with who was behind it."

"…"

"You don't believe me?"

"It's not that I don't believe you, Risya, but to be honest, there have been too many unexpected things happening…"

"Oh?"

"So I can't figure out what to believe."

The Birthplace of Witches. That was what the mad scientist Kelvina had called the research facility.

"This is the Birthplace of Witches. And it was here where I investigated the truth of this planet.

"Vichyssoise turned out well. She was the first stable subject we created here.

"Their name for the time being is Beasts of Katalisk. As you can see, they are artificial astral powers. They'll serve as next-gen energy for the Imperial forces' weapons."

The witch Vichyssoise had been created there.

But that wasn't all. The incident had also proved that artificial astral power resided within the Object they'd fought at the independent state of Alsamira.

"Risya…the researcher said that the monsters she created would be used by the Imperial forces. I know she did."

"Is that so?"

"Do you still insist HQ wasn't involved?"

"They really weren't. I wasn't, and neither was Their Excellency nor anyone else at the headquarters." Risya grinned. She narrowed her eyes until they almost looked like thin threads. "I know what you're trying to say. So now you're wondering who it could have been. To be honest, even I'm not sure."

"……Huh?"

"Well, to be more accurate, I don't have proof. I more or less *am* sure who it was, but they just haven't given themselves away yet. So this was a windfall. A perfect witch…oh, I mean mage, made her way into our nation." Risya winked.

That hadn't been directed at Iska, but at someone clinging to him from directly behind…

"Right, Princess Sisbell?"

"…"

"Princess Sisbell?"

"…I have no idea whatever you could mean." Sisbell crossed her arms and turned her face away. She knit her brows and pursed her lips, refusing to meet Risya's eyes. She was blunt and brusque. "I won't run or hide. I've even made my way to the station to go to the capital."

"Yes. Their Excellency is waiting."

"Yes, that's it!" Sisbell thrust out a finger.

She pointed at the Lord's staff officer. Had she been a soldier in the Imperial forces, she would have immediately been sentenced to disciplinary action. Though her gestures were provocative, Sisbell did not seem frightened in the slightest to address someone in a position of such high authority.

She was a Sovereign princess, after all.

"I said I would head to the capital. So why were you waiting here? Shouldn't you be there instead?"

"Ah-ha-ha. You've misunderstood, Princess Sisbell." Risya's tone was carefree. "Like I told you at the hotel, I'm accompanying you. Because of Their Excellency's thoughtful consideration for you…"

"Are you monitoring us?"

"No, nothing like that."

"So you are, then."

"Like I said, it's not like that."

This happened to be their fourth time having this same conversation since meeting at the hotel. Sisbell had not let her guard down nor made any attempt to obscure her animosity since Risya had shown up out of the blue.

...Well, in Sisbell's mind, this came out of nowhere.

...Risya did kidnap Rin with the Lord, after all.

On top of that, Risya had been targeting the witch princess with her Thread astral power. Had Rin not been protecting her, Sisbell likely would have been caught instead.

"Your name was Risya, was it?" Sisbell glanced at the Saint Disciple. "I have no intention of placing my trust in you. If I feel like it, I could look through your entire past. And if you do anything even slightly suspicious—"

"Oh? Mismis, over here."

"Are you listening to me?!"

"Well, you always draw out conversations, Princess Sisbell. It'll be okay, you'll see. Look over there. See what good friends I am with Mismis?"

Commander Mismis had gone to buy the train tickets. Risya smacked both hands down on Mismis's shoulders and started squishing her face against the commander's.

"So, Mismis, I have a favor to ask."

"What?"

"Would you lend me some money?"

"You want *money*?!"

The commander froze as Risya continued to press her face against hers.

"Wh-why would you need that?! I don't care how close we are, you can't ask for a loan. It says so in the Imperial forces' handbook…and you should have a much higher salary than me as a Saint Disciple, anyway!"

"Oh, well, you see, I don't have my wallet on me."

Risya continued to stroke Mismis's head as she stared straight at Sisbell. The princess continued to eye her suspiciously.

"So, about yesterday. Look, you remember the Lord disappeared, right? I was also supposed to head back to the capital."

"……Yes. That's exactly why I'm curious as to why you are still here."

"It seems that the Lord can only transport two people at a time."

"Huh?"

"We came together. But then the Lord headed back with Rin. So I got left behind. I must say, it took me by surprise as well."

The Lord had taken Rin and disappeared. Essentially leaving Risya behind.

"Huh? So you really are just tagging along? You're not here to monitor us?"

"Of course. I'd never lie to you, Mismis." Risya nodded and smiled. "I've had such a tough time. I was actually supposed to take Sisbell straight to the capital, so I didn't bring my wallet or anything with me. I couldn't buy myself a meal or even a drink."

"…Oh. That's why you want to borrow money from me."

"That's right. So I really need that loan, or I'm going to be in trouble. But I suppose borrowing money *is* against the Imperial handbook. In that case, would you lend me your credit card?"

"My credit card?!"

"It'll be fine. I'll pay you back double."

Risya pulled Mismis's credit card from her wallet and quickly stuffed it into her pocket.

"Oh, come to think of it, you reserved normal seats, didn't you, Mismis? Why don't we upgrade those to a first-class private room?"

"With *my* card?"

"You can submit an expense request to the Lord later."

"I'd be too frightened to even attempt that!"

"It's all right. The Lord would be nice to you since you're so cute. You're like an adorable pet, after all. They'd squeeze you just like this."

Risya hugged Mismis from behind.

"Ahh...that's so nice. You're tiny and soft and smell just like shampoo."

"It doesn't feel so nice to me!"

"Well, anyway, that aside..."

Risya swept her eyes up Mismis's left shoulder as she kept the commander in her clutches.

"...Hmm."

"What is it, Risya?"

"Well, there's something I've been curious about." Risya place a hand on Mismis's left shoulder.

"What a nice self-adhesive. You weren't caught by the astral-energy detectors at the ticket gate, I see," Risya whispered.

"Uh?!" Mismis's small body began to shake.

How did Risya know about that? Iska unconsciously swallowed his breath. Nene opened her eyes wide, and even Sisbell, who had given Mismis the self-adhesives in the first place, was slack-jawed from surprise. All of them, except for...

"So you saw through it, then?" Jhin still looked cool and collected as ever as he spoke in a stifled voice. "Still, I don't get it. If you knew about her astral crest, then why did you let us out of the Empire? And you even got us a sixty-day special leave, too."

"Oh, it's nothing to concern yourself with, Jhin-Jhin." Risya winked at him. "I mean, Mismis turned into a witch in Mudor Canyon, right? In that case, I'm responsible for what happened to her since I ordered you all to go there."

"So you even know that, too, then."

"Of course. Mismis tripped and fell right into the vortex, correct?"

"No, I didn't!"

"You didn't?" Risya looked puzzled at Mismis's exclamation. "I was convinced you'd gotten your foot caught on a rock and fallen right in."

"Someone kicked me in! The guy who was leading the enemies' forces!"

"Ah-ha-ha, how rude of me to assume. Well, I guess it's a work-related injury, then. You can get worker's comp if you file for it."

Risya let go of Mismis and gave her a jovial shake of the shoulders. It was early in the morning on the train station. She checked to make sure no one else was around.

"This is a secret. But there have been several incidents just like yours, Mismis."

"…What?"

"Whenever a vortex is found, the Empire and Sovereignty always fight over it. While it's rare, it's not as though *zero* Imperial soldiers end up as witches after being exposed to the astral energy. You see, whether someone can become a witch depends on the individual. It's not something the Empire can prevent."

They still didn't know what conditions needed to be present for someone to become a witch. For instance, Iska had fallen into the vortex, but he hadn't been affected. But Commander Mismis had. It seemed that developments like these weren't unheard of in the long history of the war.

"Oh, um, Risya!" Nene raised her hand. "Just like you said, the commander didn't end up this way because she wanted to! Um… so…"

"So please be lenient? Is that what you want to say? I think things will turn out fine. Though we can't officially reveal this, Imperial soldiers who have become witches, like Mismis, can be used as spies. They're real witches, so they can waltz into the Sovereignty."

"Is that the case with you as well?" asked the princess, who had been silent until then. She spoke in a doubtful voice.

"Risya, or whatever your name was," she added.

"Hm? What do you mean, Princess Sisbell?"

"I'm asking whether you're a witch, too. Like I am, and like Commander Mismis is."

Sisbell glared at the Saint Disciple. With a look of strong distrust in her eyes, she continued to silently face Risya.

…Of course that would bother Sisbell.

…It's even got me doubting things. I bet Commander Mismis, Jhin, and Nene feel the same, too.

The threads of astral power that had ensnared Rin. Risya had undoubtedly produced them, and she'd even owned up to this.

"R-Risya, that light isn't…"
"Oh, you mean this? That's right—it's astral power. But make sure you keep it a secret from the other Imperial force members."

Iska had been looking for an opportunity to ask about it as well. In the end, Sisbell had been the one to act first.

"You said that you're accompanying us, not monitoring us. In that case, you should tell us about yourself."

"About me?"

"That's right. Are you a Sovereign citizen?"

"No, no, I was born and raised in the Empire. Just like Mismis," Risya stated. Her answer was nonchalant, in contrast to Sisbell, who had furrowed her brows and grown deadly serious. "It's just a bonus that I can use astral powers."

"I'm asking where you got them from. Don't try to shrug it off. Would you prefer I lay your past bare with my astral power, then?"

"…"

"What's wrong?"

"No, it's just— We can talk about it, but we're still in public." Risya put a finger to her lips and shushed them with a strained smile. "I've even reserved a private car for us. Why don't we talk there?"

"You won't go back on what you said, then?"

"I would never. I know how I seem, but I'm proud to say that I've never told a lie in my life."

"That's a lie! You can't believe her, Miss Sisbell… Mgh?!"

"All righty, then, Mismis. Why don't you simmer down for a moment."

Risya clamped Mismis' mouth shut before she even finished speaking. Then she hauled the commander right onto the train. Based on that exchange, anyone could tell Risya was rather adept at kidnapping people.

"All right now, please come this way, Princess Sisbell."

"Truly suspicious..."

"I can assure you I'm not. My creed is 'Sincerity, integrity, and charity,' after all."

"Another lie! Risya always says that and then goes off and decides to... Mgh?!"

"Quiet now, Mismis."

She was dragged away, still gagged. Iska and the others reluctantly got on the train to head after her.

3

Nebulis Sovereignty, Star Spire.

Alice was walking fast through its halls.

"Ugh, I can't believe the meeting finished thirty minutes late. What was wrong with Lord Mask? 'Your queen proxy outfit is stunning, it makes you look very elegant.' What was that about...?"

It had been when the conference of the three bloodlines had ended. Normally, Lord Mask would immediately leave with Kissing, but he had called out to Alice as *she* was about to exit.

Her queen proxy outfit...

Alice had worn her personal clothes until recently. Now,

however, she was wearing the attire of the queen's official proxy. She did this to show she did not intend to give up the queen's throne. Though her outfit had been constructed in the same style as her previous royal dress, it featured more florid red and blue hues.

...What did that mean?

...Lord Mask didn't comment on it at the last conference.

So why now?

Alice felt an ominous chill run down her spine when she realized Lord Mask hadn't pointed out the outfit until now.

...Is he up to something?

...He was in an oddly good mood, too. I can't help but wonder about it.

She couldn't let her guard down. She knew for a fact the Zoa and Hydra were vying for the throne. The Hydra had targeted the current queen's life, and Alice knew they were also responsible for bringing the Imperial forces into the Sovereignty. Under normal circumstances, she would have immediately accused them of those crimes.

"But I need proof for that. I need Sisbell to come back..."

The room in front of her eyes...

The Lou queen's personal quarters, the Stardust Skyscraper. Though these chambers belonged to her mother, she was unfortunately still consulting with the ministers after the conference. Alice pushed open the doors in place of the queen.

"...I've just barely made it."

She glanced at the wall clock and let out a sigh of relief. But just as she did that, the light of the communications device on the table lit up.

"Huh?! A call!"

She scrambled to pick it up. Alice leaned forward and pressed the monitor close to her face.

"Sisbell! It's you, isn't it, Sisbell?!"

"I'm sorry for making you wait, dear sister. I was a few minutes later than expected."

A girl with strawberry-blond hair came on screen. They had only spoken through a voice call the day before, but this time, Alice could actually see her sister's face. Was she inside a building?

It was clean, but the walls that surrounded Sisbell looked like those of a cell.

"Oh, are you wondering where I am? I'm in the restroom of a limited-express train."

Sisbell glanced around, checking to make sure no one would overhear.

"Just as I said yesterday, dear sister, I will be heading to the capital to rescue Rin. Actually, I am already *on my way there. On this train."*

"So you were serious…"

Alice was conflicted. Rin was irreplaceable to her, and she would have done anything to rescue her attendant. But on the other hand, she also wanted Sisbell to return home immediately.

Neither option was better than the other.

Her desire to help her most beloved attendant was at odds with her wish to keep her sister out of harm's reach.

…The capital is the most dangerous part of the Empire.

…Going there is like heading toward the witch hunters.

Sisbell was walking straight into the lion's den.

The capital would have astral-energy sensors installed everywhere. If her sister was captured for being a witch, it would all be over.

"…"

"Oh? You look as anxious as the others."

Alice couldn't tell whether Sisbell understood her current anguish.

Sisbell answered, fully calm and collected. *"This is our chance to counterattack. If Rin and I are safe, no one can do anything to us anymore. Rest assured we will unveil how the Hydra made a barbaric attempt on the queen's life and kidnapped my attendant."*

"I know… But how are you making sure *you're* safe?"

"Me?"

"That's right. I'm afraid of what will happen if you're caught before you can rescue Rin."

"I have guards I can rely upon."

Sisbell produced a picture. She brought it close to the screen so Alice could see, which made Alice doubt her own eyes. It was a picture of Iska and her own sister walking close together, arm in arm.

"Do you see, dear sister? This is how close we are."

"Ngggh?!"

The picture had likely been taken in an urban area in the Empire somewhere. Iska and her sister were strolling, arms linked, shoulders pressed against each other boldly despite the looks from families and businesspeople surrounding them.

It was almost as though…

Almost as though they were a couple on an afternoon date.

"Wh-wh-what do you think you're doing, Sisbell?!"

"We pretended to be on a date while surveying the enemy domain. It is an Imperial city, after all."

Sisbell waved the photo around, showing it off. What flagrant, indecent behavior.

"That hour was so perfect. I feel so at ease near him. Just feeling his strong, muscular arms fills my heart."

"Iska probably hates it! He obviously looks uncomfortable!"

"I feel content, so that's what matters."

"What are you talking about? Iska is my rival... Guh...!"

Alice hadn't told Sisbell about her relationship with Iska. She did know, however, that Sisbell had an inkling of it.

...No, she's fully aware!

...She's defying me because she knows!

Sisbell was trying to steal him.

But he's my rival, just mine—

"Hee-hee. I'm sorry, Sister, but the battle has already been decided."

"...What did you say?"

"Our difference in experience is showing."

Sisbell put the photo in her pocket. Then she placed a hand against her cheek and turned her warm, glistening eyes upward.

"Iska and I have already done so many things together. Just thinking about it makes me blush..."

"Wh-what did you do?!"

Alice howled at the image of her blushing sister on the comm before glaring at her through the screen.

"Y-you couldn't have! I don't believe it! Iska...would never be baited by someone like you into doing anything scandalous!"

"Scandalous?" Sisbell was taken aback. She blinked. *"My. I never said anything about doing anything indecent at all. Nothing of the sort."*

"Huh?"

"I walked around holding Iska's hand and took pictures with him, and we had a drink together at a café. That was what I was reminiscing about."

"......What?!"

"Oh my."

Sisbell brought her face closer to the camera. She was grinning derisively, as though to say, *I got you.*

"Oh, dearest sister, what in the world could you have been imagining? Pray do tell me—"

Snap.

Just then, something shattered in Alice's mind.

"Oh, sister."

"Shut up!"

She abruptly turned the comm off. When Alice came back to her senses, she realized the call with her sister was over.

"Oh..."

"How was it, Lady Sisbell?"

"I-I'm so sorry, Shuvalts!"

She quickly turned to the older gentleman waiting in a corner of the room.

"I was hoping to let you talk with her after..."

"I am grateful for your consideration of me. However, through her voice, I was able to hear she is doing well, even from here. As her attendant, I am relieved."

Shuvalts was Sisbell's attendant. He had been confined to the Hydra's astral power research institute, the Snow and Sun, until escaping a few days ago.

"But still..." Shuvalts glanced at the comm on the table. "I was a bit surprised to hear those details from you, Lady Alice. Was it Iska you spoke of? I am shocked that his unit would still help Lady Sisbell even after returning to Imperial territory."

"But didn't you negotiate with them to ensure her safety?"

"Yes, indeed. But that was originally for their time in the independent state of Alsamira. Although..." He paused for some time. "I didn't think they would be so faithful about keeping up their end of a verbal promise... It seems there are reasonable people even among the Imperials."

"That's right! Indeed, my amazing Iska is—"

"Hmm?"

"...Never mind."

She casually turned away.

That had been too close. Since Shuvalts was also an attendant, Alice had almost let it slip as though she were talking to Rin.

"But, Shuvalts, please make sure to educate my sister. She's forced her bodyguard into doing such odd things."

"Ha-ha-ha," the gentleman laughed. "Oh no, Lady Alice, that was simply a little sister poking fun at her older sister. She is not yet at that age. And he is an Imperial as well."

Oh, how naive he was! How truly naive!

In her mind, Alice balled her hands into tight fists. She recalled when she had searched her sister's room. Though her sister had very serious books on history and culture lining her shelves, Alice had found teen romance novels hidden among them.

...She's the type who is only book smart about these sort of things!

...She simply acts as though she's innocent in front of Shuvalts!

Sisbell knew even more than Alice about what went on between a man and a woman. Alice could tell from seeing that picture with Iska. She could see it in the way her sister had so blatantly wrapped her arms around his, how Sisbell had so calculatingly made sure their skin touched in such a nonchalant way. Her sister was, without a doubt, attempting to seduce him.

"..."

Whew. She took a deep breath.

"As I thought, I need to hit where it hurts."

"Exactly. We cannot allow the Zoa and Hydra to continue without repercussion."

"...That wasn't who I was referring to."

"Huh?"

"Oh, it's nothing."

Alice shook her head, attempting get back on track.

Even if she were to use Sisbell, who was attempting to steal Iska, as a model to learn from for her own "education," Alice couldn't afford to get distracted by what was happening in the Empire.

She needed to keep a close eye on the Zoa and Hydra.

"Shuvalts, would you be kind enough to accompany me for a while?"

"As you wish. Though I am older, I will do all I can to be of service to you in Rin's absence."

Alice had no attendant, and Shuvalts had no lady to attend to. Because they were each lacking their counterpart, they had temporarily constructed a rapport.

Then...

The door opened behind them.

"Oh...Your Majesty!"

"I'm sorry for the delay, Alice. The ministers do keep the conversations long when they catch me after a meeting. They wanted to make small talk and kept going on and on about a cat that messed up the lawn... I really should have cut off the discussion there and come back faster if I'd known they would be wasting their time on that." She walked into the room with a sigh. "Alice, did you get word from Sisbell?"

"Yes. She is more detestable than I imagin— Oh, I mean, she seems to be doing well. Like she told me yesterday, she is going to the capital to save Rin."

"...I see." The queen sighed yet again. "It seems quite the complex situation. Though as her mother I wish she would return home immediately, I feel somewhat elated to hear this news."

"Because she's attempting to save Rin?"

"Yes. I never thought she would volunteer to do anything of the sort."

The queen smiled wanly, seeming worried.

"She holed herself up in her room and hadn't shown herself for days or weeks. I cannot believe she would leap at the opportunity to enter enemy territory of her own volition."

"Like mother, like daughter, Your Majesty," Shuvalts said. As he was preparing drinks at the table, he paused. "I am quite sure Lady Sisbell inherited her tomboyishness from you, Your Majesty."

"...I did cause you quite a lot of trouble three decades ago."

The queen's face slackened into a smile.

"How are you feeling, Shuvalts?"

"I apologize for worrying you, Your Majesty. While I was confined to the Snow and Sun, my perception of time was so warped it felt like weeks...but as you can see, I am back on my feet."

"I see. I wanted to ask you more about that."

Her lips tightened into a thin line. She looked at Alice and Shuvalts in turn.

"You were restrained by a Hydra assassin and confined within the Snow and Sun."

"That is very much true."

"And you were freed by..."

"Him," Shuvalts replied heavily. "...By Salinger."

"Salinger... You...freed me..."

"Just to pester them. I don't care why you were trapped in Snow and Sun, but I'm sure losing their captive will hurt."

The transcendental sorcerer Salinger.

Alice had heard that the felon who disappeared from the thirteenth state of Alcatroz had, for whatever reason, attacked the Hydra base. Why had the sorcerer saved a butler of the royal family?

"Shuvalts, did he say anything at all?"

"No. He only asked me what the Hydra were planning. It seemed that he only freed me to ask this."

"...I see."

The queen closed her eyes as though lost in thought, like she had lost herself in some faraway scene.

"Salinger, what in the world are you—"

Her mother stopped—there was a sudden rumble from below their feet.

"An earthquake? B-but this one is...much larger!"

Shuvalts stumbled.

"Your Majesty!"

They could barely stand.

The floor was practically swaying. Alice grabbed her mother's hand and squeezed it tight. In the center of the living room, mother and daughter clung to each other for support. They heard glass cracking in the halls.

What could have been shaking the palace?

"A—a giant earthquake?!"

"...No, Alice. Something very similar to this has happened before... It couldn't be!"

The queen held Alice as her eyes went wide.

"She couldn't possibly be awakening!"

4

The limited-express train.

The continental railway connected the eastern reaches of the Empire all the way to the distant Imperial capital. In a private compartment of the train...

"Oh! So this is your astral crest, then, Mismis. Well, it's very striking."

"R-Risya, don't say that so loud!"

"Looks like big chests mean big astral crests."

"What are you talking about?!"

"Ah-ha-ha. Sorry, sorry. But the doors are closed, so it should be fine."

There was a faint green astral crest on Mismis's shoulder.

Risya was observing it with great interest and speaking in a carefree tone as she did.

"...Seriously." Mismis placed the self-adhesive on her left shoulder again and fixed her sleeve. "Well, I've shown you mine, so where's yours, Risya?"

"Hm?"

"We were just talking about it earlier. We all saw you use your astral powers."

Mismis stared. She raised her eyebrows as she silently looked at Risya, who sat to her right.

"Yes, that's right," Sisbell joined in.

Risya was sandwiched between Mismis and Sisbell.

Across from her sat Jhin and Nene. And Iska was closest to the door.

All five sets of eyes were concentrated on Risya.

"......Hm. Right."

Risya crossed her legs and glanced at Sisbell.

"I was actually planning on having Their Excellency explain."

"Are you still trying to feign ignorance?"

"No, no, that's not my intention at all." Risya played things off with a smile when Sisbell glared at her. "Well, Mismis and the others know already. I guess I'll just say it since the Sovereignty is aware now. We were researching *that* in utmost secrecy within the Empire. We were trying to make artificial crests form on humans."

Risya put up two fingers.

"We were researching two ways of accomplishing this."

One, the old type, which would create an astral crest without accompanying astral powers.

Two, a new type that would result in both a crest and powers.

"Oh!" Nene yelled and stood up.

"Is that the thing from when we went to rescue Iska?! You gave me and Jhin artificial crests!"

"Right, that thing… That was back when we were headed to Alcatroz, right?"

Jhin grimaced. "We used a weird device to give ourselves crests when we were trying to get across the Sovereignty border. You said that just one shot on our skin will turn us into a witch, right?"

"That's right. But the artificial crests are so much more useful if you can utilize astral power," Risya said with a wink. "Nene and Jhin-Jhin, your crests were part of the first experiment. The one I tried was the second. Needless to say, we've designed them so they disappear after use. I can use astral powers for just a week before they disappear with the crest. So, Princess Sisbell?"

"…What is it?"

"Do you know why? Do you know why the astral crests we administer disappear within a week?"

"…" The Sovereign princess sighed slightly. "You are bestowing astral energy, not astral power itself. Because if you were using real astral powers, you would end up becoming a real witch just like Commander Mismis there."

"What a prompt reply! That's correct!"

"Are you making fun of me?"

"No, no, that was a sincere compliment. I would have expected no less from a witch princess." Risya crossed her arms, seeming satisfied. "It would be very useful to wield astral powers indefinitely, but keeping astral power in your body turns you into a witch. I can't afford that as an Imperial."

"I have a question, too," Sisbell said, talking over Risya. "How much do you know?"

"Me? About what?"

"When did you learn Commander Mismis was a witch? And you knew who I was when you appeared with the Lord."

"It's just as you say."

"Were you watching us this whole time?"

"Oh, now you've misunderstood me." Risya shrugged and joked. "I didn't follow you or watch you. Their Excellency just happens to have that power."

"The Lord does?"

Sisbell looked even more grim—her sentiment shifted from dubious to cautious.

"What does that mean? Can the Lord look into the past like I can? Or is it clairvoyance, where they can see anything happening in the present?"

"It's not quite that." Risya tried to hold back a yawn. "Their Excellency's sense of smell is just slightly more sensitive to the movements of astral power than normal people's. Though that doesn't mean the Lord will find all the information they want. Actually, it's quite the opposite. There's something they cannot look into, in fact."

"And so that's why you've set eyes on me. What are you planning on making me do?"

"The Lord would like to extend to you an invitation..."

Risya held out a hand. Sisbell pulled back in response, but Risya put her arms around the princess's shoulders as though they were old friends.

"Won't you become a Saint Disciple, Princess Sisbell?"

"E-excuse me?!" It wasn't Sisbell who shouted this, but rather Commander Mismis, who had been watching the exchange the whole time. "Hold on, Risya! What's going on here?! Um, Sisbell is a Sovereign princess. And she's a witch… Iska, can witches even become Saint Disciples?"

"I'm not sure…"

In fact, that was a question he himself had wanted to ask. He had been so taken aback by the unexpected proposal that his mind had gone blank from surprise, and he was at a loss for words.

Sisbell? A Saint Disciple? Was that an *actual* invitation to a princess from the Paradise of Witches?

"…I don't understand."

Even Sisbell looked almost dumbfounded.

"Are you asking me to become an officer within the Empire? To betray the Sovereignty and pass along intelligence in order to obtain a high rank within your nation? Then the answer is obv—"

"Well, that shows how open-minded Their Excellency is."

"Huh?"

"That is how courteously the Empire would welcome you, Princess Sisbell. What Their Excellency seeks to learn has nothing to do with the Sovereignty's secrets. It's about the Empire."

"What about the Empire?"

"Well…"

Risya's only response was a cool smile.

Her smile was directed at the members of Unit 907.

"Now, this is a place Isk has fond memories of, I'm sure. There's an Imperial assembly deep underground in the capital. Isn't that right, Commander Mismis?"

"…Uh, well, yes. I don't know much about it, though."

"Why, of course you wouldn't. We can't go around just telling any Imperial soldier about it willy-nilly. There are only a handful of people in the Imperial forces' headquarters who know where it actually is."

Behind the lenses of her glasses…the eyes of the staff officer to the Lord—of Risya—narrowed.

"It's the first place in the world where a vortex formed, after all."

"…What did you say?!"

Sisbell stood up. She couldn't contain herself. The information Risya had just uttered was something she desperately wanted, more than anything.

"But why did it happen in the Imperial capital?

"The events that took place a century ago. I don't imagine that the surge of astral energy in the capital could have simply been a coincidence."

Sisbell had said that at one point. A century ago, a vortex had formed for the first time on the planet in the Imperial capital, by "coincidence." The massive amounts of astral energy that showered upon the people in the area created the first witches and sorcerers. Sisbell wanted to see the past events for herself.

"So are you taking me to the Imperial assembly, then?"

"That's exactly right, Princess Sisbell. What the Lord wants to know is located there. But there's a rather troublesome issue."

Risya slipped off her glasses. As she twirled them around the hinge, she looked around at the members of Unit 907.

"We always seem to be interrupted by a certain *nuisance*."

"A nuisance?" Jhin's face darkened. Next to him, Nene, Commander Mismis, and Sisbell all looked puzzled.

"Huh! The Imperial assembly… You don't mean that!" Iska

felt his neck break out into a cold sweat, and an enormous chill ran down his spine. He couldn't believe the enemies they'd be up against would be— "Risya, you can't mean…"

"That's right. There are people who lead the Imperial assembly. If we're taking Princess Sisbell there, they will have friends who will block us."

The corners of Risya's mouth lifted into a daring smile, her glasses still off.

"The Eight Great Apostles themselves."

"Huh?! Wait, you can't mean…," Jhin started to say.

"Now, now, settle down, Jhin-Jhin. It's all right. My life is on the line just as much as yours. So let's try not to die, shall we?"

"…Not exactly reassuring, is it?" Jhin said, clicking his tongue.

Nene and Commander Mismis had gone silent. In that oppressive atmosphere, Sisbell hesitantly spoke up, even though she likely had sensed the disquieting mood.

"Um…Iska? Who are these Eight Great Apostles…?"

"The Imperial assembly is just a *cover*." Risya beat him to the punch. She put her glasses back on and pointed down at her feet. "There's something slumbering deep below the capital that the Eight Great Apostles don't want anyone to see. So they built the Imperial assembly down there to hide it."

"…Risya. What is it that they're afraid of people seeing?"

"That's what Sisbell here will show us, Iska." Risya clapped Sisbell on the back. "I'm expecting great things out of you, witch princess. Well…I can more or less guess based on the data from Kelvina's lab. Now I just need to see it for myself and then— Oh?"

Risya blinked in surprise. She reached into her pocket as everyone stared at her. She had produced a comm.

"It's a message from HQ. Hmm. I already *know* I neglected to attend that meeting earlier......... Princess Sisbell."

"What is it? Go ahead, you can tell me."

"They say there was an earthquake at the Sovereignty."

"......Come again?"

"But they didn't observe any geological movement," Risya said. "It's not a vortex, either. Do you know what that could possibly mean?"

Risya put her comm away.

Her expression showed slight irritation, which was rare for her, and something Iska was seeing for the first time.

"...She's awakening now of all times. This is such a drag, Your Excellency."

INTERMISSION

Those Who Intuit It

1

The Castle Tower Seat.

Despite its rather ostentatious outward appearance, the fortification had little in the way of protection. Save for a small number of office workers and electricians, there was no staff, nor were there any guards. Instead, the building's security was handled entirely by defensive mechanisms.

Other than the Saint Disciples, a very select few were allowed to come and go as they pleased. And as for who these exceptions were?

They were simply those the Lord had given permission to wander the building.

"You tricked meee!"

Rin's angry voice echoed throughout the Lord's chambers as she sprinted through them, her hair sopping wet. Small droplets of water dripped from her face and neck. For whatever reason, she was only in her underwear—a situation she would normally never be caught dead in. To cut to the chase, she had just come out of the bath.

"Hey, you beast! What was it you were saying about getting cleaned up?!"

"Weren't you the one who said you wanted to wash off your sweat, witch?"

The silver-furred beastperson was lying on the tatami. Lord Yunmelngen glanced at Rin in her underwear.

"You're the very first person from the Sovereignty I've ever allowed to wander through these halls. You should be happier."

"Sure, I got to the bathing area, and even got to use the shower."

"You see?"

"But why are there security cameras *in* there?!"

She had undressed and taken a quick rinse. Just as she'd been about to step out, Rin had realized a tiny camera was installed on the shower nozzle.

"Were you recording me naked?!"

"Well, you are a hostage. I need to watch all your movements, don't I?"

Lord Yunmelngen rolled over. In their hand was a small security monitor that showed a feed of the shower room.

"Don't worry. I'm the only one who saw you in the buff."

"Oh, that makes it *so much* better!"

"Ha-ha. I must say, I wasn't expecting to find your astral crest *there*."

"Don't laugh! What's so wrong with having an astral crest on your butt?!"

Rin stomped firmly on the tatami. She knew that the beast-person she was talking to wouldn't be easily intimidated by that.

"You Peeping Tom!"

"I am simply observing a human being."

The Lord sat cross-legged on the tatami and stared at Rin from head to toe. She'd run here in her underwear because she'd scarcely given herself enough time to put on clothes.

"Huh."

"Your ogling is creeping me out."

"Then hurry up and put something on."

Though Rin was being rather harsh, the beastperson was laughing. Their shoulders shook.

"I haven't seen an undressed human in a while. I mean, look at me. I'm close to forgetting what I looked like as a human."

"..."

She put on her housekeeping clothes.

Rin faced the monster in front of her again. She looked at the Lord's fur-covered limbs and thick fox-like tail. From this distance, there was no mistaking them for a human.

"Will you tell me already what you are, beast?"

"What's that supposed to mean?"

"I don't want to, but I'll believe you are the Lord for the time being."

But why would the Lord look like that? And what was this about 'being human'?

"So you're saying you used to be human?"

"Half, at least."

Lord Yunmelngen pointed at his own temple.

"I'm mixture of human being and astral power."

"What?"

"You asked whether I used to be human. The human part of me will answer yes, but the astral power inside will say I used to be an astral power. Anyhow, both aspects are now melded together in spirit."

"How odd..."

"The same holds true for the Founder Nebulis."

"What?!"

When she heard the Lord say that, it wasn't the Founder, but the transcendental sorcerer Salinger whom she recalled.

"The tri-stage, the integration of humans with the astral powers.

"But only two have reached that state using their own power in the history of the world."

The fusion of human and astral power. And the complete version of it was right before her eyes.

"So this is what that is!"

Cold sweat broke out on her forehead. How had she not realized it until now? That the words Salinger had so heedlessly spoken would come back into her life with such monumental meaning?

"...Lord Yunmelngen." Rin struggled to say the words with her dry mouth. "So you used to be human, too. Then...did something turn you into this? Is the Revered Founder the same as you? Is that why she looks the same even a century later?!"

"..."

Sitting cross-legged, the Lord looked up at Rin. They then stared up at the ceiling.

"It's not that I dislike my body or my soul. But…who wouldn't feel irked at not knowing who made them this way?"

"……? You didn't transform of your own volition?"

"I have my suspicions about who did this to me."

The beast smiled. Sharp canines poked out from their mouth as the Lord sneered ferociously.

"That's why I want the witch princess Sisbell. She has the power to revive the memories of the planet—and I need to find out who made me the way I am."

2

The Imperial assembly. Also known as the Unseen Intent.

Its name originated from the legislative building having never been noted on any map.

It was over three miles underground, below the capital. The temperature was 302 degrees Fahrenheit. Even microbes could scarcely cling to life at these depths. The underground lair was so deep, it escaped the prying eyes of the Nebulis Sovereignty…yet that was not the true reason it had been built here.

It was because this place was the closest to the original vortex.

The Imperial assembly functioned as its cover.

It had been established as an observation base so no one from the Nebulis Sovereignty or the Empire could approach it.

"The witch princess has left the eastern region of Altoria."

"Only two more stations, and she will arrive at the capital by sundown tomorrow."

The spacious parliamentary hall.

The monitors set up on the walls within the assembly hall displayed the hazy outlines of eight people.

The Eight Great Apostles.

They were the supreme leaders in charge of the assembly. In place of the Lord, who was not directly involved with the government, these people effectively had full authority over the rule of the Empire.

And these eight...

...were astir.

"Risya is traveling with her along with the Successor of the Black Steel, Iska."

"Risya... Of course."

"The Lord has certainly become aware that we know Their Excellency is assisting her. And is aware of our involvement in the incident of that day."

The witch princess Sisbell was approaching the capital. And Lord Yunmelngen desired to know the truth of what had happened a century before at the vortex.

However...

...that would be most troublesome for the Eight Great Apostles.

"We have done our part to erase evidence of our involvement a century ago in relation to the astral energy eruption."

"The witch princess..."

"If we can simply eliminate her, the Lord will never know the truth."

*　　*　　*

"Surreptitiously…"

The assembly fell silent.

The monitors had shown the outlines of eight men and women, but one of them had abruptly disappeared.

Only seven figures remained.

Had they witnessed this, the lawmakers of the Imperial assembly likely would have doubted their own eyes and wondered what in the world had happened.

"Luclezeus has headed over."

"This will not hinder our progress. We need only eliminate the witch princess and the Successor of the Black Steel. The depths of the planet await our arrival— What?"

Zwish.

A static sound rippled through, and the images of the Eight Great Apostles glitched. Was it an electromagnetic disruption? No…

"A massive amount of astral energy?"

"It originated from an area below the Nebulis palace in the central state. But the burst of astral energy was too sudden to be a vortex… It couldn't be…"

The Eight Great Apostles were astir yet again.

An unparalleled, immense wave of astral energy had made its way across the great distance to the Imperial capital.

"This is…"

"Is it you, Founder?"

CHAPTER 3

The Day of Revival

1

The Founder, Nebulis.

In the past, she had turned the Imperial capital into a sea of flames. She was the strongest and oldest astral mage. Though the Empire called astral mages witches, she was the one they called the Grand Witch.

"The most bloodthirsty rage in the world. Such strong feelings of resentment, enough to annihilate the Empire."

Lord Mask looked up, unable to hide the jubilant quiver in his voice.

It had all been so much. It had all happened so suddenly. After tremors that had set the underground lake in motion, a girl had awakened before his eyes.

"The Revered Founder..."

Only shards of broken glass remained of the coffin. The

fragments were continuously fluttering through the air in the massive current of astral energy, almost like a snowstorm.

"Beautiful..."

The color of the energy shifted from red to yellow, then to green, then to blue.

In its light, a tanned girl slowly rose from the casket, her pearlescent hair fluttering.

"It is an honor to be in your presence, Revered Founder."

Lord Mask knelt on a knee and lowered his head before her.

This was most definitely the Founder. Though the astral energy had already begun to fade, it was doubtful anyone would question who she was after seeing the divine energy she had released upon her awakening.

"............"

The girl stood before Lord Mask.

Her slim sun-bronzed figure peeked out from her worn cloak. From appearances alone, she seemed as if she could be only thirteen or fourteen years of age.

The Founder swept her gaze across the underground lake.

"This is the subterranean level of the palace...?"

"Yes, indeed."

Lord Mask nodded deeply.

He could not hold back the crescent moon–like smile that bloomed below his mask.

Why now? Why had she, the most powerful astral mage in existence, awakened now of all times?

That didn't matter.

What mattered was retribution—revenge against the Empire.

For the Zoa, whose greatest desire was to rescue Growley, understanding the mysteries of the Founder did not matter.

All they needed were her emotions.

As long as they both had rage fueled by their desire for revenge against the Empire, that was enough to suit the Zoa's needs.

"I apologize for not introducing myself earlier. I am On, the adviser of the house of Zoa."

"Zoa?"

"Your sister, and the first generation of our family, was blessed with three children. At present, we are divided into three bloodlines: the Lou, the Zoa, and the Hydra."

"…" The Founder was silent.

In contrast to her youthful appearance, the expression on her face was complex and mature.

"I do not care…"

"I fully share your sentiments. To you, O Revered Founder, the current monarchy is a trivial matter."

He stood up. Lord Mask bowed to the small girl and snapped his fingers.

"I will gather the family posthaste. We shall serve your every—"

"No need."

"Then what will you have me do?"

"…"

Her pearlescent hair fluttered around her as she glanced at Lord Mask.

"I will do it alone. I will burn the capital to the—"

"Stop right there!"

*　　*　　*

A sweet voice echoed throughout the rocky cavern.

Then they heard footsteps.

"......Ugh."

A golden-haired girl ran toward them, out of breath, and Lord Mask clucked with his tongue.

The tremors had been massive. He'd had the suspicion someone would show up, but he hadn't expected *her* to be the first to arrive.

"Well, I wonder what could be the matter. Why do you look so upset?"

He did not show any indication of annoyance on his face, instead welcoming her with the best smile he could deliver.

"My dear Alice."

———————

Twenty minutes ago.

"...Huff...ugh... Why now of all times?!"

Alice ran down the steps of the queen's palace, panting.

The elevators were no longer functioning. The Nebulis palace was the Planetary Stronghold. Although the lifts ran on astral energy rather than electricity, they had abruptly stopped functioning.

...The astral energy in the entire palace is on the fritz.

...This didn't happen when the Imperial forces attacked, though!

It had all started with the tremor.

The quake that seemed as though it would overturn the very ground itself had begun to disrupt the astral energy flowing within the palace.

"Are you sure it's the Founder...? Your Majesty!"

The queen was not here. She had entrusted her daughter with the reconnaissance work as she stayed behind to give instructions and control the situation in the halls. That was why...

Alice had to run.

"This is no laughing matter! We cannot allow *her* to awaken again!"

She knew because she had seen it once before. The Founder Nebulis was no friend to the Sovereignty and would never be the Sovereignty's savior. The Founder was a calamity, a prisoner to revenge.

"I will annihilate the Empire."
"I am a witch, and you are my enemies."

The Founder cared about nothing but destroying the Empire.

She wouldn't bat an eye, no matter how many sacrifices there were and no matter who was hurt, Imperial or not. That was who Founder Nebulis was, who that witch was.

...But that's wrong. It's wrong!

...That's not the future I want!

Alice needed to stop her.

"Rin..."

If only her attendant were by her side, Alice would feel so much more assured. She bit her lip as she ran down the steps to the underground level.

She descended a hidden path only the royal family was allowed to traverse. Opening up ahead of her was hard rock face and water that glittered bright blue.

The underground lake.

The queen had designated it as the place to seal the Founder away again.

The moment she set foot in it...

...Alice felt an intense burst of light and wind that made her voluminous golden hair stand on end.

"A current?!"

Based on the ferocity and vast size of the blast, it must have been astral energy that was full of rage.

She understood that, whether she liked it or not.

What had happened here? What terrible events had led to this?

"Stop right there!" she yelled, her voice raspy.

"Well, I wonder what could be the matter. Why do you look so upset?"

A man's sonorous and melodious voice echoed throughout the cavern. The man wearing a mask greeted Alice with open arms as she struggled to catch her breath.

"My dear Alice."

"Lord Mask..." She glared at the man in front of her. "Is this your doing?"

"Mine? Oh, no, you're quite mistaken. The Revered Founder herself willed this to be."

He gestured at the broken coffin. In the center of the fragmented glass stood a girl whose iridescent hair fluttered.

Blank.

That was how Alice would have described the vacuous eyes staring back at her.

"The Founder..." She was too late. Alice bit the inside of her cheek when she saw the girl was already up. "It's been a while, hasn't it...?"

"…"

The Founder was silent.

Or so Alice thought—instead, the girl averted her eyes as though she hadn't seen Alice. She began to scale the rock face on her bare, slender feet.

"Uh! Stop right there!" Alice cried. Her loud yell echoed throughout the underground lake cavern. "Founder Nebulis, I will not allow you to leave!"

"…" The bronzed girl stopped.

It was almost as though time itself had halted. Or that was how it seemed as the girl slowly, languidly almost, took her time turning to face Alice.

"So it's you."

"It's an honor you remember me," Alice answered. "And I remember how much trouble you created last time you were awake."

Rin had been cut down as she tried to protect Alice. Embers had rained down on the neutral city of Ain as though from the ravages of war. The image had been forever engraved in Alice's mind.

"Are you planning on destroying the Empire…?"

"What else is there for me to do?"

"I wouldn't have a reason to stop you if that were all there was to it."

The girl was so much smaller than Alice, and looked even younger than Sisbell. Regardless, the witch's mechanical gaze was enough to send a shiver down her spine. Its depths were endless. How much power and how much hatred could be contained in such a tiny body?

"As the current proxy to the queen, I implore you! O Founder,

your rage will not lead to the Sovereignty's future. You cut down your own allies to destroy the Empire!"

She balled her hand into a fist.

"We don't need your powers."

She pressed on, taking a stand against the oldest and most powerful witch there had ever been. Though she felt so overwhelmed she could hardly breathe, Alice strained her voice regardless.

"I will unify the entire world. In different way from you!"

"…"

A long silence followed. Alice's voice echoed against the rock face and disappeared like the ripples of waves. How much time had passed?

Hmph. A lifeless sigh escaped the tan girl's lips.

"Begone, girl."

In that same moment, crimson flames engulfed Alice's vision.

2

Imperial territory.

Twenty-first Glasnacht.

They were within sixty miles of the Imperial capital, the last stop of the limited-express train.

"Ahh, I'm so tired…"

Mismis, who was splayed out on a bench in the station, let out a long sigh and rolled over.

"Even a nice private car is tiring when you're being rocked around all night by a train… The capital is so far away…"

"It's right in front of us," Jhin said, standing next to the bench Mismis was lying on. He glanced at the train stopped at the platform. "After we leave this station, it's straight to the capital."

"…Huh?"

As he watched the conversation out of the corner of his eye, Iska glanced around the terminal. Only Commander Mismis, Jhin, and he were in the station area. Nene and Sisbell, who had been with them, weren't present. And Risya was gone, too.

"I don't see the others, Commander."

"Oh, Risya said she had something to do, so she left the station. She said she would come back before the train leaves."

"Then what about Sisbell and Nene?"

"…I'm…over here…"

Sisbell, who was looking rather pale, alighted from the train.

She was leaning on Nene's shoulder and looking as sick as an employee suffering from a terrible hangover after a night out. She staggered and teetered on her way over to a bench.

"…It's motion sickness… Oh, Miss Nene, I'm so sorry for imposing."

Then she collapsed onto the bench—incidentally, falling on top of Commander Mismis, who was still sitting there as well.

"Gah?!"

"Oh…Commander Mismis. What are you doing lying about here? Someone might sit on you. You must be careful."

"You already *have* sat on me! Your butt was right on my face!"

Commander Mismis leaped up. Just then, the comm in her handbag rang softly.

"…Huh? Who is it from?"

It could have been headquarters. Or perhaps Risya, who was outside the station. Though that was what Mismis thought, when she brought her face up to the screen…

"Yes, this is Mismis—"

"You're late. You haven't arrived at the capital yet?"

"Yeeeek?!" Mismis's voice cracked as she jumped back.

She almost flung the comm into the air with the force of her leap. It was little wonder she did this, because the person on the other end wasn't actually a human.

It was a silver-furred beastperson.

Of course Commander Mismis would be surprised to see that.

"Uh…ngh…um, uh…well!"

"Ah-ha-ha. Did I frighten you? Am I really that scary looking?"

Lord Yunmelngen.

Despite their uncanny appearance, Lord Yunmelngen seemed to be in a mischievous mood and found her reaction fairly entertaining.

"And Princess Sisbell is coming, right?"

"I—I am right here!"

Sisbell, who had been sitting down, opened her eyes wide very suddenly. She brought her face close to the screen, almost as though she were taking the Lord in through her eyes.

"I won't run or hide! We're due to arrive in the capital soon… um, uh, yes, right. We're currently at the twenty-second Glasmach."

"You mean the twenty-first Glasnacht. You got every bit of that wrong."

"Sh-shut up, Jhin... More importantly, Your Excellency?"

"What is it?"

"Is Rin all right?" Sisbell ground her teeth. "I have heard you desire my powers. For this trade, I have one condition. You must ensure Rin's safety—"

"I'll show her to you right now."

"Yes?"

The screen switched over—to a certain brown-haired girl sitting next to the Lord.

"Rin?!"

"Lady Sisbell!"

"Rin, are you safe?!"

"I'm not being manhandled here. I've been released from my handcuffs as long as I stay in this room...but."

Rin clenched her jaw as she faced Sisbell.

"I am not pleased about being made a plaything. Lady Sisbell, you needn't worry about me. Please prioritize your well-being fir—"

"There, checkmate."

"What?! Why, you little—!"

On the other side of the camera, there was some sort of commotion, and the screen turned back to the Lord.

"That's thirty-one wins for me. Really, you're all bark."

"Why, you little—! You coward! How dare you move the pieces while I was talking to Lady Sisbell! How on earth are you the leader of the Empire?"

"Ahh... You really don't know how to insult people, do you?"

"What did you say?! Again! I'll wipe that grin off your face this time—"

"Rin?"

As she looked at the prisoner beyond the screen, Sisbell sighed loudly. She looked absolutely exhausted.

"You seem awfully relaxed for a captive. The train is about to leave, so I'm going to hang up now. I hope you remain this spirited."

"See, what did I tell you? You don't need to worry at all, Princess Sisbell."

A can of soda in hand, Risya slowly made her way over.

"Oh, you can hang up now. I'm sure you've noticed that the captive is doing well enough on the other end."

"......Yes. She was doing so well, it was somewhat of a letdown."

She tossed the comm back to Mismis and sighed.

"I almost feel like leaving Rin behind and returning to the Sovereignty."

"Now that would be an issue. Come over here."

Risya gestured to her to come close. She was pointing at the stopped train on the platform...or rather, at the ticket gate beyond it.

"I rented a car. So let's get going."

"Excuse me? What do you mean?"

Sisbell ignored Mismis's complaints and gave a sharp gaze to Risya.

"Aren't we headed to the capital? We should only be a few hours away by train."

"Yes, that's right."

"Then where are you planning on taking me in that car?"

"Ah-ha-ha-ha, why are you acting like I'm a villain?" Risya

dismissively waved her hand. "We *are* heading to the capital, of course. I just have a little stop to make on the way."

"Where?"

"..."

Risya snickered. The Lord's staff officer couldn't hold back her mean-spirited smile.

"Do you remember Kelvina, that mad scientist who had you held captive?"

"How could I forget?"

"What would you say if I told you she had another laboratory?"

"What?!"

"We'll talk in the car. Oh, come now, Isk, don't look so grim. Or you, Jhin-Jhin, Nene, and Mismis."

After saying only that, Risya walked out of the ticket gate in high spirits.

"Wh-what should we do?"

"There's nothing to debate about," Jhin answered Sisbell in a wearied tone. "We've got an errand to run before we head to the capital. I'm sure this is one of the Lord's conditions, so he won't mind the excursion."

"I'm not very interested in doing anything except saving Rin." Sisbell crossed her arms. "It's creepy that she still has research facilities around. Her research is sacrilege to the astral powers. I cannot turn a blind eye as a Sovereign princess, so I must crush them to smithereens. And by 'I must,' I mean Iska must, of course."

"Me?!"

"I'm not any good at fighting. So I must count on you."

"How nice to have an excuse, I see."

"All right, we're off!" Sisbell gallantly walked forward.

Following after her strawberry-blond hair, which lightly fluttered behind her, Iska walked through the station's ticket gate.

An hour later.

They were in the back seat of the rental car.

"Risya, or whatever your name is…"

"What is it, Princess Sisbell?"

"Where is this hideout? After being jostled about in the car for over an hour, all I see around us are skyscrapers."

"I suppose it must be disguised, then. It's probably hidden in a building."

"Probably…?"

"I just found out about it earlier, too, from a message. Oh, Nens, turn right at the crossing about a hundred yards ahead."

Risya was sitting in the shotgun seat, giving instructions to Nene, who was driving.

"Look, Mismis, do you remember? There were all sorts of suspicious computers in the underground area of the research facility you guys found."

"Oh, right! But we didn't have time to look at them since we were searching for Sisbell."

"You were right to avoid touching them. If you had gotten the password wrong, the whole place would have exploded."

"Eep?!"

"So we mobilized the Imperial forces' Intelligence Service. They very carefully retrieved data from the computers—"

"And figured out there was another hideout. And that's where we're headed."

Jhin was staring out the car window. His silver hair, which was smoothed back, ruffled as the wind rushed through the half-open window. "But what's going on with the rest of it, Saint Disciple? You've got to have an idea of how dangerous the research facility is, right?"

"..."

"So?"

"I think it'll be bad."

"......Hm." Jhin raised his eyebrows.

Though she spoke casually as usual, there was an unusual heaviness to her words.

"What does that mean?"

"Oh, you're a lifesaver, Isk."

She looked at him through the rearview mirror of the car.

"Give it your all when you fight. I'm not really well equipped for battle, even if I'm part of the Saint Disciples."

"I'd really rather not..."

"Oh? And why's that?"

"..."

The question didn't require an answer. They would need a Saint Disciple's abilities in combat. That implied a foe who Risya could not handle alone was lying in wait.

This was what she meant by "bad."

Mismis and Nene, and even Sisbell, who was not an Imperial soldier, all went silent from the tension.

...But what's waiting for us?

...Was Kelvina researching something else?

Research that could turn humans into witches. Experiments that could turn humans into fallen angels. And the artificial astral power called the Beasts of Katalisk.

Was there something more? Was there something that even set Risya, the Lord's own staff officer, on edge?

"...This is useless to talk about," Jhin said, sounding annoyed. "So, Saint Disciple? Where exactly is this facility supposed to be?"

"Right in front of you. Oh, Nens, turn at that intersection and head straight. Just keep going straight a hundred yards."

"Sure... Uh? Wh-what's going on?!"

Nene hit the brakes as soon as she turned left. She'd barely done it in time. Had she been even a few seconds too late, the car would have plowed through an Imperial forces' barricade.

"Th-the Imperial forces?!" Sisbell yelled when she saw the imposing wire lattice of the barricade.

An armed unit of soldiers stood there with anti–astral power riot shields at the ready. There were dozens of them, and they were surrounding the place.

"All right, all right, Princess Sisbell, don't worry about them. They're just here to dissuade people from wandering in. We can't have rubberneckers, after all, and no pesky reporters or cameramen, either."

Risya gallantly hopped out of the car. She gestured for them to follow, and the others piled out.

"Uh... Are we really leaving the car?"

"I-it'll be all right, Miss Sisbell... I think." Even Mismis, who held Sisbell's hand as the princess shrank away, had a twitch in her smile.

Though the Imperial soldiers were her colleagues, Mismis was currently a witch. If they picked up on this with the astral energy sensors they had...

"Okay, we've kept you waiting long enough."

Risya strolled up to the Imperial guards with enough buoyancy to clear away the mental state Iska and the others were in.

"Captain Rondle, any word from HQ yet?"

"Yes. We've set up the surveillance cameras around the plant and its surroundings. We won't let even a bug escape our watch!" The captain saluted. "We opened the door in the back of the first floor at ten twenty. I have my men on standby so they can storm the place at any moment."

"Thank you very much. So, about that"—she glanced at all the forces in the area, then winked at Iska's unit—"this is the investigation squad I've got with me. They're Unit 907, affiliated with Special Defense Third Division. The same unit that fought and fended off the Ice Calamity Witch in the Nelka forest. We can rely on them."

"Yes, ma'am."

The dozens of eyes from the armed units turned to focus on them. Iska, Jhin, Nene, and Commander Mismis. Though they were all dressed in their civilian clothes, the introduction had revealed their identities.

"Who's the girl, ma'am?"

"Eep!"

The witch princess hitched her shoulders when the captain looked at her.

"She doesn't look like she's affiliated with the forces."

"Hee-hee. Curiosity got the best of you, Captain?" Risya placed a friendly hand on Sisbell's shoulder.

Then she said, in a very mischievous tone, "This is top secret, but this girl is Lady Sisbell, granddaughter of the Lord."

"What?!"

"Huh?!"

The captain's eyes opened wide.

Sisbell's face turned red as lava.

"Y-you cretin! Wh-who are you saying is the granddaughter of that furry inhu— Mgh?!"

"Settle down now, little girl. Can't have you yelling." Risya had placed a hand over Sisbell's mouth, and she whispered into her ear, "You're the Lord's granddaughter. She will be referred to the Imperial headquarters in five years. So we're having her come as part of her on-site education. And I came here on official business as the Lord's staff officer, so I'm your instructor."

"…"

"What a good girl. Now keep quiet like you have been, if you please." Risya winked but kept her hand over Sisbell's mouth. "So, Captain, Their Excellency has recommended her to the Imperial headquarters, and I've been ordered to ensure she receives on-site experience."

"I—I see! I extend my apologies!"

The captain and his subordinates retreated in a hurry. Like the sea parting, the barricade of force members opened up.

"Well, looks like we're off on an adventure, everyone."

"You haven't heard the end of this…" Sisbell followed after Risya, muttering under her breath. Then Unit 907 followed behind them. They headed down the road originally blocked by the soldiers.

"How about I tell you a story, then?" Risya, at the front, said as though she'd suddenly remembered something. "The Imperial capital was burned to the ground by the Founder Nebulis's rebellion a century ago. The cities around were terribly damaged as well."

"Why are you telling us this now...?" Sisbell's tone was sharp. "Are you trying to say the Empire was the victim a century ago? In that case, I'll have you know that we astral mages were discriminated against by the Empire fir—"

"It's still here. Now, what do you think I mean by that?"

"Hm?"

"What I mean is that the factories here were abandoned after being ravaged by the flames of war. The Imperial capital has cleaned up nicely, sure, but once you leave it, you'll start finding factories from the past that have remained untouched."

Their view opened up. Ahead was a large and expansive open area.

"Um...Risya?"

An abandoned factory.

Commander Mismis scowled dubiously and pointed at the demolition flyers posted on the concrete walls.

"This building looks like it's already set for demolition. If this really were an important research facility, they wouldn't tear it down."

"Kelvina's computers identified this location as one of her labs."

Risya headed into the overgrown field grasses and walked to the back door. The double doors had been wrenched open and crushed in the process. The faint smell of gunpowder had likely come from the armed unit's attempt to break the lock of the sturdy entrance.

"Incidentally, after headquarters looked into some things, they discovered that this place was marked for demolition a decade ago."

"...What?"

"Leaving an abandoned factory as is would make for a good disguise, right?"

They entered the quiet building.

Unlike the facility that Kelvina had used as her home base, it was surprisingly bright inside from the rays of light that filtered in from the domed ceiling.

And there was nothing in it.

It wasn't really a factory so much as a large, empty warehouse.

"Um…but there's nothing here?" Sisbell looked down at the floor, which was carpeted thickly with dust. "The place where I was imprisoned was equipped with many computers and strange furnaces that emitted astral energy."

"Let's see what you can do, Princess Sisbell." Risya produced a comm. She looked over messages that seemed to have come from headquarters. "Forty-three days ago, at two in the morning. The surveillance cameras on the street we walked down earlier caught an image of a woman who appeared to be Kelvina entering the factory."

"…"

"We have an exact time. You should be able to reproduce it with that, yes?"

"So that's what you wanted…" The witch princess placed a hand on her chest. She undid the first three buttons of her top and peeled off the adhesive that had been placed under her clavicle. Faint astral light spread throughout the factory.

"O planet."

Light like a projector gathered in the empty space and recreated the figure of certain person, apparently the woman witnessed coming to this factory.

"Please show me your past."

"I was waiting for you."

*   *   *

The researcher Kelvina.

Just as when they had met her in the eastern jurisdiction of Altoria, her rouge hair seemed as though it hadn't been combed in years, and she wore a white coat over her shoulders.

To borrow Risya's words, this was Kelvina from forty-three days ago.

"To be frank, I was hoping to never see her face again." Sisbell bit her lip.

The illumination of the astral power continued the projection. Next, men who seemed to be involved in transportation appeared. Two men carried gigantic containers one after another into the warehouse according to Kelvina's instructions.

"Be very careful with it, now. These are precious materials. If you drop one and break it, I'll use you as subjects for my experiments as compensation… Oh, that was just me mumbling to myself.

"Back here."

Thunk.

When Kelvina pointed at the wall of the factory, a dent appeared.

A hidden passageway. The space between the two walls contained a stairwell that led to the basement.

"Oh. Well now, this is a useful power." Risya's voice betrayed her wonder. She looked at the projection before her, then at Sisbell.

"Well, that's frightening, actually. With a power as useful as this, I bet the Nebulis Sovereignty and retainers were afraid of the intelligence you could gather."

"…"

"Oh, said too much." Risya stuck out her tongue. "But thank you, Princess Sisbell. Next, Isk, if you could handle the wall—"

He didn't need to be told. Iska quietly used his unsheathed black sword to slice through the inner wall. It broke apart. On the other side of the crumbled wreckage they found the stairs leading underground. Just like in the projection.

"Now, how about we get going?" Risya headed down the stairs at a rhythmic pace. Sisbell followed, then everyone else.

The hall was filled with monitors.

Iska and the others had set foot in a large room packed full of small and large monitors along every wall. There were hundreds—no, thousands of them. The ceiling and side walls were no longer visible because of the great number of screens attached to their surfaces.

All of them were turned on. An endless stream of green text flowed from top to bottom on every single monitor.

"This is bizarre. It's nothing like the lab in Altoria."

"......Right." Iska nodded slightly at Jhin's comment.

What was this place?

...Is it not an astral power research facility?

...It's completely different from Kelvina's other research facility.

"A giant furnace was set up.

"This faint bluish-green light poured from the furnace."

Kelvina's previous lab had been drawing astral power and energy from an underground vortex and proliferating it through enormous furnaces.

But what was happening here? They didn't see any furnaces to speak of, nor did they see ducts to transport anything. The countless monitors buried the walls, and the cables that extended from them were as entangled as tree roots as they draped along the ground.

"You don't think this is an observational facility, do you?"

It had slipped out. Nene looked up at a large monitor on the wall and quietly whispered, "Risya, may I try using this keyboard?"

"That's fine with me, Nens."

"All right, then…"

Nene's fingers seemed to dance over the keyboard as she typed something out. She was putting together strings of formulae and letters Iska couldn't hope to comprehend. After she had inputted dozens of lines…

"Seventy-ninth report record."

Above their heads, on a screen as large as a movie theater's, a report popped up…

"To the Eight Great Apostles.

"Transmitting samples of reappearance of Astral ■ ■.

"It was a joyous day. Through the witch transformation of Subject Vi and the better-than-expected results of Subject E, my hypotheses have been ninety percent confirmed.

"My hypotheses regarding the fusion of humans and astral powers."

"We call those possessed by astral power witches and sorcerers.

"We have known about this phenomenon for a century. However, I

have identified that the astral energy we collected forty-seven years ago from the polluted region of Katalisk contains a curious impurity."

"Something similar to astral power, but not quite the same.

"It seems to be in the nature of the substance to exist in people already possessed of astral power. In other words, the person is possessed by two entities. Unfortunately, because it is selective about its host, there are few who are compatible.

"Those who are can apparently gain powers far greater than any normal witch or sorcerer.

"In exchange for this power, however, the individual must undergo a physical transformation.

"These are my so-called subjects. This is deeply intriguing."

"This is…" Jhin's brow furrowed as he looked up at the text on the monitor. "Are they referring to that monster Vichyssoise from the Hydra family? So she didn't end up like that from being possessed by astral power, but because something else possessed her?"

"I think that's how we should interpret this," Nene said hoarsely while nodding.

Commander Mismis, who was next to her, and even Sisbell were standing stock-still, unblinking as they stared at the display. Only one person here was composed.

"Risya."

"Hm? What is it, Isk? Why are you looking at me like that?" She turned to him. "You have a question for me?"

"How much did you already know about what's shown on this screen?"

"I knew all of this. The Lord does as well."

Iska had thought she would dodge the question, but instead she'd readily answered.

"What I want to know is everything that comes after this."

"After this…? So, Nens, come on, keep going!"

When Risya pushed her to move on, Nene became flustered but turned back to the keyboard and said, "R-right."

As before, she typed something out.

"This is how I understand this phenomenon.

"Humans and astral powers create what we call astral mages.

"When an individual combines with astral power and a different third factor, an astral mage will transform into a new being.

"The witch Vichyssoise is an example of this… However.

"At our present stage of research, we have only been able to reach three cases of complete compatibility."

"Lord Yunmelngen is an amalgamation of astral power and the planet's defensive wishes.

"The Founder Nebulis is an amalgamation of astral power and the planet's interceptive wishes.

"And Subject Elletear is a union of astral power and ■■ *(what the Astrals feared and called the Great Planetary Calamity)."*

"Let us continue our research.

"We must catch up to those three. Elletear's fusion is particularly far along. She is transforming into this planet's final witch.

"We must carry on our investigation into Katalisk.

"V, E, L, A, P, N, O, and W have all consented. We have detected several coordinates for the city of ten billion stars, Reinenhabe, where

■■ *slumbers. We must hasten our transition plans for five years into the future…"*

The feed cut off.

The report that had been displayed disappeared, and the monitor was once again flooded with cryptic text.

"So that was all of it, then…," Commander Mismis hesitantly said. "Vichyssoise was mentioned, so I knew the Hydra were involved, but it still feels unsettling. And the Lord and Founder were also mentioned. But I'm not sure what those letters were at the end. Risya, is this what you wanted to know—?"

"I found it."

"What?!"

"Vittgenshla, Etienne, Luclezeus, Alleten, Promestius, Novalashlan, Ovan, and Wizeman," she announced as smoothly as a song. Risya stated the names she had learned by heart as she faced the commander. "That's what those letters are, Mismis."

"What are?!"

"They're the initials of the Eight Great Apostles' names. V, E, L, A, P, N, O, and W. They match, right?"

"……Huh?"

"That was one of the things the Lord and I wanted to know. Coming all the way here was worth it."

Risya turned around on the spot. As though to say she had no other business being there, she turned her back to the gigantic screen.

"It's just as the report says. There's a reason the Lord ended up in that form. But Their Excellency never asked for it. To prevent another tragedy like that from ever happening again, the Lord

OUR LAST CRUSADE OR THE RISE OF A NEW WORLD. VOL. 10

forbade all ordinary citizens from experimenting on astral power within the Empire."

"What?!"

"Didn't expect that, did you, Princess Sisbell?" Risya looked down at her. "Astral power research is forbidden in the Empire because astral power is a wicked thing—I'm sure that's what the Sovereignty has told you."

"A-are you saying that's not the case?!"

"The Lord has never said such a thing." Risya shrugged as though joking. "The Empire only restricts civilian research on astral power. The reason astral power research was limited to Omen, which is under the Lord's control, and why it is restricted to certain areas, is to prevent such things from happening again."

"Th-then what was Kelvina's research?!"

"She was going against the Lord's morals."

"......Tsk."

Sisbell sucked in a breath.

That was how much cold anger was imbued in what Risya had said.

"And we've finally figured out who was behind it all. Through those initials. The eight of them hid their true colors. But we've finally unearthed proof of their treachery. Now we just need to extract this data and head back to the capital..."

"This is the end of the line."

They heard someone's staticky voice echo throughout the hall. It had come from the giant monitor they had all been looking at. The text flowing down the screen disappeared, and a humanoid silhouette took its place. It seemed to creep up from within the screen.

"Risya, Sovereign witch Sisbell. And the Successor of the Black Steel, Iska. You will never reach the capital. This cold basement is the end of your journey."

"What?!"

"Oh, come on, you've seen this before, Isk. You've seen him on the Imperial assembly's monitors."

"......Huh?"

"This is one of the Eight Great Apostles. Though this my first time seeing him outside of that screen, too."

Risya narrowed her eyes behind her glasses.

A hazy hologram, almost ghostlike, rose from the ground. There wasn't an ounce of goodwill in her eyes as she looked upon it.

"Based on your voice, you must be Luclezeus. I'm surprised you'd make a trip out all this way from the Imperial assembly. Is the record I've discovered that dangerous?"

"Indeed."

"You sure were quick to confirm that."

"There is no use trying to hide it from you. You can deduce many things from just knowing one piece of information, and I'm sure you've gleaned many more from that report."

"So you rushed over here to destroy the evidence, then, I presume?"

"I'm not here to destroy the evidence. I'm here to destroy the witnesses."

At Luclezeus's words, Iska felt a chill run down his spine. The Eight Great Apostles. They were the supreme authority who had led the government and military in all respects.

...I just realized something.

...The Lord and the Eight Great Apostles are at odds with each other behind closed doors. And they have been since the very start!

The Eight Great Apostles had been conspiring behind the Lord's back, and Risya had come all the way here to find proof.

"Well, I'm sorry to tell you, Apostle...," Risya began, feigning disappointment. She shrugged, but her eyes were just as sharp as before. "I don't mind that you got so worked up and came all the way here, but as for that holographic form you've taken... Your body has already rotted in the hundred years since then, so I'm sure you abandoned it."

"Our souls will walk this mortal plane again."

Roar!

From behind the hologram, the monitors on the wall fell one after another to the floor like a blizzard. Then the blank wall that remained was ripped apart and separated into two. Amidst the wreckage stood a gigantic furnace that bellowed out steam.

"Iska! It's the same as the ones in Kelvina's underground facility!"

".......Right."

Next to the on-guard Sisbell, Iska unsheathed his astral swords. Steam that contained the divine light of astral energy belched from the furnace. Something was inside.

"It's the Object's successor."

The furnace broke apart. From behind the steam that had blown away the thick wall of metal, they could hear the ground groaning under heavy footsteps.

"A beast?! No... Is it a mechanical soldier?!"

"In Kelvina's words, it is part astral power, part machine— an astralnomical soldier. In place of machine hardware, we've bonded astral body parts throughout its form."

It was a pseudoliving robot that walked on two legs. Though it was still an automaton, it was covered in slimy snakelike scales, and its legs were as strong and muscular as a lion's.

And it breathed. Its whole body lifted and lowered as it took breaths in like a real creature, and the way it bellowed out astral energy–laced steam was exactly like that of a living being.

"We, the Eight Great Apostles, abandoned our bodies a century ago. And now we seek a vessel for our cyberbrains."

The hologram disappeared. Almost immediately, a bright light illuminated the mechanical soldier's eyes.

"And this is our vessel. The astralnomical soldier shall house my soul."

In a word, the robot was a silver Object. The giant, which expelled steam from between its mechanical parts, spread its arms like a person.

"All that's left is to find a fitting energy source."

"Oh, now that I didn't expect. You want something more, even after getting such a ridiculous body?"

"Astral energy isn't enough to sustain it."

The Apostle's quivering voice, emanating from the soul controlling the soldier, rang out.

"That was how it was a century ago. We searched for an energy source that went beyond steam or electricity to run these soldiers. In other words, we once sought astral power...and now, at long last, we've found it—something to surpass even that!"

"...Huh." Risya didn't even raise an eyebrow. "I suppose the Lord did mention something like that. But that substance can't be controlled by just anyone."

"It depends on how you use it. That which slumbers at the planet's core is the ultimate energy we seek. It captured the mad scientist's interest, after all."

"So now what? You plan to rebel against the Lord with that power?"

"The age of astral power will end."

His footsteps made the very ground shake. Luclezeus's upper body moved as his lower half crushed the monitors without leaving vestiges underfoot.

"I will tell you about one of the things Kelvina was researching here. She experimented on containing astral power. Do you understand, witch?"

"Huh?" Sisbell stood on guard when he addressed her. "What are you trying to say?"

"Astral power inhabits humans. It cannot possess inorganic steel. But we would never have enough energy to start up the astralnomical soldiers unless we made that happen. So, if it wouldn't possess steel, then all we need to do is trap it inside. We'll seal away the astral power into the machinery."

"You don't mean the Object is..."

"That's exactly right. This is the result of our initial experiments. We sought to turn astral power into an energy source."

Astral power passed through metals by nature. So they'd simply needed to trap the astral power in a cage that would keep it in place.

"As the astral power attempts to escape, it releases energy.

We use that to fuel the astralnomical soldier. And as for why I'm telling you this…"

The floor split. The four corners of the room cracked apart, and crooked blackish-brown towers sprouted like living plants from the ground.

"…that applies in this case as well."

False Barrier—Planet's Nucleus.

The room began to transform. Instead of rising to the ceiling, the steam from the furnaces began to whirl and eddy.

"A barrier that the Founder once used to hide her astral power as she fled the Empire. You may think of it as an isolated area where astral power is sealed away. But by enveloping this room, astral energy can neither enter nor escape."

"I see… So you were careful to prepare in advance."

Risya glanced around.

Four towers stood in the four corners of the room. The light they discharged from their tips surrounded the place. That must have been the barrier containing the astral power.

"No astral energy will be able to leave these walls, then," Risya said. "Meaning the Lord won't be able to sense there's something wrong?"

"Yes, the Lord can sniff out the stirring of astral power, can't they?"

This barrier sealed away the "odor" of astral power. If the astral power could not escape in the form of a "scent," the Lord would remain unaware of the fight happening underground.

In other words, the Eight Great Apostles could act right under their nose.

"Successor of the Black Steel, Iska, you did well to keep the Ice Calamity Witch at bay in the Nelka forest."

"Tsk."

"However, you unintentionally came too close to unearthing what lies at the center of the world. That is your crime," Luclezeus declared. "And we have heard from Talisman about you, Sovereign witch, Sisbell. That your power would be of great assistance."

"What did you just say…?"

"But you are working with the Lord to uncover the events of a hundred years ago. That is your sin. And Risya, staff officer to the Lord."

He looked down upon the humans at his feet, who were much too small in comparison to the astralnomical soldier.

"You have been incredibly useful until now."

"Yes, yes. So what? What's your accusation against me?"

"That you chose the Lord instead of us. The Eight Great Apostles were waiting in anticipation for you to betray the Lord and come to us."

"Ha!" She laughed. "Unfortunately, I will remain faithful to the Lord until the very end. Once you've fallen in love with that fluffy tail and come know how soft it is, you wouldn't be able to betray them, either."

"How very laudable of you."

Luclezeus's pronouncement of their deaths made the very ground groan.

"This is your last stop. Now return to the bowels of the planet."

CHAPTER 4

The Planet, the Vessel, and the Soul's Oratorio

1

Red as blood, infinitesimal as snow.

The embers fluttered.

"...Wall!"

The faint embers almost seemed like a mirage. She saw them enter her vision; Alice had unconsciously created an ice wall.

A cinder burst, and great flames bloomed from it. The water in the underground lake evaporated. The bedrock below broke and exploded, sending clods of earth and sand up into the air. The sounds of the blasts hit her eardrums, nearly knocking Alice unconscious for a moment.

"...She's...showing no mercy!"

She gritted her teeth and forced herself to stay conscious even after nearly fainting. She shouted into the flames that engulfed everything before her eyes.

"Come out, Founder! I haven't been hurt in the slightest!"

"No mercy? And here I was thinking I was being exceedingly charitable."

The swirling flames disappeared as though they had simply been a bad dream.

"This can be seen as kindness, considering you're an ice astral mage, after all."

"You call this kindness?" Alice said. "Anyone other than me would have been charred to a crisp."

"But I used it on you, so it is."

From beyond the dying flames, a little girl stood barefoot atop the charred ground, a serious expression on her face.

"I saw your astral powers," the girl continued.

"If you decided I'd be able to survive this, I suppose I should consider that an honor. But what do you intend to do to everyone other than me?"

Lord Mask was nowhere to be found. He had been standing between her and the Founder, so she hadn't had the time to protect him with an ice wall.

...Any person engulfed in those flames wouldn't leave a trace behind.
...Even Lord Mask.

Alice had a sudden premonition.

"Founder, the man standing there was one of your great-grandchildren. And you—"

"A gate astral mage need only teleport prior to the explosion."

So that was it.

Alice clicked her tongue at the unexpected turn of events. Though they would have both been engulfed in flames had they been a second too late to react, in the end, she and Lord Mask had both survived by a hairbreadth. But that was hardly different from pure luck.

And the Founder called that being charitable, ancient tyrant that she was.

"..."

Alice looked around again. The once-bountiful well of the lake had evaporated, and she was now standing in a vacant underground hole.

Alice and the Founder. The two mages were illuminated by the faint light from the bedrock. There was likely a vortex under them. The astral light had seeped into the minerals and glittered like jewels.

"Founder."

She stared down the girl wrapped in a worn cloak.

"I will say this as many times as I need to. You're going to burn the Empire to the ground, aren't you? No matter how much damage it does to the Sovereignty and neutral cities?"

"I don't intend to answer that again."

"Yes. But I'll keep asking as many times as I need to!"

She pointed at the girl—at the living proof of their persecution a century before.

"I won't ask you to suppress your anger. But if you were to unleash it, you won't be the one who gets hurt. It'll be everyone weaker than you!"

"..."

"Your old values have no place with the people who live in the modern day!"

"Then here is how I answer."

The Founder Nebulis flipped her right hand, her palm to the ground.

"Do you know how much blood, how many tears we shed to create the Sovereignty? You know nothing of its history. You were simply born into royalty, so what kind of world do you even aspire to build?"

"Tsk… Those are fine words coming from you."

"What do you know of peace when you've never experienced the age of despair?"

The ground rose. Four obsidian-black spires towered around Alice.

"What?! What is this…?"

"Enclose."

The Founder snapped her fingers.

Black light spread from the four spires and engulfed Alice from all around.

Readvent Barrier—Planet's Nucleus.

Sizzle…

"Ouch!"

The moment Alice touched the black barrier with her fingertip, sparks appeared. She couldn't help but yelp when it scorched her skin.

"This is the end," she heard the Founder say.

"Don't underestimate me. I don't know what this barrier is, but don't think you can keep me locked away behind a curtain!"

Alice created an ice dagger in her right hand to cut the curtain.

She started to slash at the black barrier around her with the blade. And it worked. But then the blade of ice disintegrated.

"......Huh?"

The dagger hadn't broken, but rather, the ice crystals made from her astral power had crumbled and vaporized into nothing. Was it due to the high heat? No. If that were the case, it would have melted. It was as though something had corroded the astral power itself.

"It's a cage that seals away astral power," she heard the Founder say from outside the barrier.

Alice couldn't see the Founder because of the dark curtain, but it was obvious whom she was addressing.

"The black rock accumulates astral energy. It absorbs any type of astral power, so once a mage is surrounded, they're rendered powerless."

"What did you just say...?"

The dome of black light. The ebon spires must have been the source of the barrier. So were they made from stone that could store astral energy, then?

"A century ago in the Empire, we didn't have your stickers to hide our astral crests. So we created barriers to conceal ourselves. But you can also think of them as cages for containing astral mages."

"This is...a cage?"

The concept wasn't unknown to Alice. For example, the self-adhesives that mages used to cover their astral crests were made from something called Nebula, a substance that neutralized astral energy.

...But this is on an entirely different level.

...It can absorb any astral energy, no matter how powerful?!

In other words, it was the ultimate nullifying prison. Any mage who was surrounded by it could never escape. She had been trapped. She couldn't believe the oldest and strongest mage would use such underhanded means.

"You coward! Let me out!"

"How unsightly."

She could feel the Founder's contemptuous glare from beyond the curtain.

"Sit tight. Wait until the moment I turn the Empire into a sea of flames."

"...!"

"You're useless without your astral power. Someone like you could never change the world."

Before Alice could make a sound, the place where she stood was buried in complete darkness.

2

"The era of astral power will soon end.

"The superior power slumbering within the planet's core will reform the world."

An astralnomical soldier—a biped that was half astral power, half mechanical giant. Iska had no time to speculate about what the silver Object was made of, nor how it had come into being.

There were two things he and the others needed to be careful about. One was that Luclezeus's soul had possessed the astralnomical soldier. And at that moment, that very Apostle was their enemy.

"The Eight Great Apostles shall usher the planet into a new age."

The giant thrust out a hand. A cross opened on its palm, and a geyser of steam shot out along with a flood of what looked to be astral light.

And that illuminance... The moment they saw it condense into one spot, Unit 907, Iska included, all yelled, "Run!"

Jhin ran toward the back. Nene and Mismis each ran to the opposite side. Meanwhile, Iska reached toward Sisbell with enough force to push her down as he took cover on the ground.

"Nightgaze."

A bolt of light shot out with a screech and scorched through the air.

It hit the place Sisbell had been standing only a moment ago. Had Iska not pushed her out of the way, the light would have certainly vaporized her.

...The intense flash of light.

...It's the laser that the Object called Life Form Integra!

The astralnomical soldier had released the very same beam from its gigantic palm.

The frightening thing was that it hadn't taken long for the energy to collect for an attack. There was no delay between the light converging and its being discharged.

...Can I cut that with my astral sword?

...I'm not confident I can. Even if I could, I'm sure I'd only have a one in three chance of pulling it off.

If he missed, he would be shot. Perfectly cutting such a large beam of light would require nothing short of a miracle. Even with Iska's skills, the odds weren't in his favor.

"Sisbell, get back!"

He had her take refuge close to the wall, then held his ground. Continuing to dodge the attacks would be impossible. He needed to find a chance to counter—immediately.

"There's no way you can. You'll never have a chance to counter-attack me."

Luclezeus grinned coldly in his current form. The Apostle held both his arms aloft in front of him. A cross-shaped fissure spread across not only his right palm that had just shot Nightgaze, but also his left.

"Two at once?! You can do that…?"

"Iska, you were able to intervene only because I was aiming at the witch. So this time I'll take care of you both at once. Only one of you can survive now."

His hands stretched out toward them. Hot steam surged out of the two fissures as astral light began to condense.

"It's you or the witch. Choose who should live and who should die."

"You brute! Are you suggesting that I'm nothing but a hindrance to him?!" Sisbell roared.

As she placed her left hand on her chest, the Illumination astral crest glowed brightly.

"Who do you think prevented the Object's sensors from working in the independent state? Just try to see through the illusions my astral power can create… Wait, what…?"

Sisbell froze. Nothing had appeared. She had conjured a sandstorm in Alsamira. By using the dense cloud of sand, she had been able to confuse the Object and misdirect its shot. Now, however, she wasn't able to produce the mirage.

But the astral power was glittering on Sisbell's breast.

"Wh-what is going on…?!"

"What a pitiful creature you are. It seems this witch isn't very smart."

Luclezeus thrust his hands before him and sighed.

"I told you. This barrier cuts everything off. Outside astral power cannot affect this area. So what do you think that entails?"

"You don't mean…?!"

"That's right. This proves to be a most inconvenient situation for your astral power. Because you've been cut off from the astral power's information, you can't read the events of the past."

There was nothing she could reference to revive. Even when engaged, Sisbell's astral power could find nothing to recreate.

"But…?!"

"You can take your rage with you when you become one with the planet."

Nightgaze.

The lasers unleashed from his palms headed straight for Iska and Sisbell. But they didn't hit their targets.

Instead, the astralnomical soldier's body lurched back.

Luclezeus lost balance and his arms flew up. The lights pierced the room's ceiling instead of Iska and Sisbell.

"Oops. Sorry, but the Lord has taken a liking to the princess."

"…I see."

Luclezeus took a knee as he tumbled back.

There were several threads thinner than hairs tangled around his knee. Except it wasn't just his knee. They were around his throat and shoulders as well. The thin, glistening strands bound him until he was immobile.

"I thought you were being rather quiet for all your talk, Risya."

"Well, you were just so passionate about your little act, Luclezeus. I was simply trying to avoid butting in. That's all."

"So that's the fourth-generation Thread astral power..."

"Yes. I'm surprised you'd know it. It should have been hidden from the Apostles by the Lord's decree."

Risya was holding a small orb of light. It unraveled in the air and turned into threads that covered the hall like a spider's nest.

"The barrier prevents astral power interference from outside. So self-sufficient powers can be used without issue within the room." Risya gave her wrist a half turn. "In which case, constrict."

Creak.

The threads wrapped around Luclezeus's head and began to dig into his throat. Though they were thin as hairs, the strands of astral power had captured the multiton giant. Due to the steel machinery, his body was able to withstand it, but the threads likely would have been able to immobilize a hundred human men.

"Y-your astral power is amazing, Risya!"

"Hee-hee. Isn't it, Mismis? It's really handy." Though she said that, the smile didn't reach Risya's eyes. "I'm able to use Thread by extending threads made of astral energy and constricting them, that's all. But once you've been caught in my web, I've won. It doesn't matter how strong you... What?"

Snap.

Something broke. Risya's threads floated to the ground as they were torn to shreds.

"Planet's Crust."

The ones around his neck, shoulders, and knees disappeared.

After regaining his freedom, the silver giant slowly raised his head as he sat up.

Curved blades glinted from the backs of his hands.

"They're made from the same crystal as the Planetary Stronghold. There is nothing they can't cut. Even string made from astral power."

"I see... So that was how you did that to my threads," Risya murmured. "They seem a little too sharp to me. Those cords should have easily been thirty times stronger than steel wire of the same thickness..."

"You're next."

"No thanks!"

Risya scowled as she leaped back. Without a moment's delay, Luclezeus stomped toward her. He was just a stride away. For every three steps she fell back, he took one to catch up. He lifted his fist over his head. The crystal blade glinted in his hand.

"I pass judgment upon you."

He thrust the blade at Risya's chest in an attempt to skewer her. But before he could...

"You're slow, Isk."

"Hragh!"

Iska intervened by reaching her just a moment earlier. He slid along the floor between the giant's legs and brought down his black astral sword to protect Risya.

They heard something hard break.

Iska's blade had perfectly broken Luclezeus's.

"...The astral sword. I knew it was bad news!"

The giant took a step back.

Iska didn't even give him the time to leap away. He brought his sword down again, tearing into the giant's breast armor. It broke apart, and Iska sliced through the cables within that were likely the machinery part of the giant until he saw a glitter of light.

It twinkled faintly and cryptically, almost like an illusion.

"Astral light?!"

"N-no, it's not, Iska! That's astral power itself!"

The witch princess's eyes went wide. She knew because she had been born with astral power. That was the source of the astralnomical soldier's strength. The internal mechanisms of the robot were a cage for astral power.

"You...you demon!" Sisbell bellowed, baring her teeth.

Never before had she trembled like this, even when she had been afraid for her life. Not once had she ever trembled with *rage* like this. The witch princess moved with a fervor that Iska had never seen.

"You call us witches and sorcerers...yet here you are, under-handedly, wickedly using astral power for your own ends!"

"____"

"This is sacrilege to the planet! Release the astral power!"

"Why, of course."

The armor Iska had sliced through reconstructed itself. It had only taken a few seconds. The astral power prison also disappeared from view.

"I told you. The era of astral power will soon end. If we can simply obtain control over that which slumbers within the

planet's core, astral power will be a useless tool to us. We will be able to release it immediately."

"But I'm telling you to release it now!"

"Then we will make a deal."

Strong astral light once again flooded from his joints. The giant slammed his fist onto the ground.

"In exchange for your life, witch."

His fist smashed through the floor. It created a shock wave like that from a tank's shell, and a giant fissure opened in the ground.

Bedrock Bloom.

The pattern on the ground took on a bright lava-red hue as countless circles, large and small, appeared one after another within the large room. Within each circle, eddies formed, and scorching wind began to swirl.

"This is...?!"

Iska had seen this before. The sorcerer Salinger had called one of his similar attacks Terra Burst.

In which case...

"This is bad. Get away from the red rings!"

"What? Uh, um..."

"Miss Sisbell, jump!"

Nene charged at Sisbell when the witch hesitated. The moment she was tackled to the ground, the circles around the room burst with bright-red flames that reached the ceiling. It was like the eruption of a volcano.

"Ouch... Th-thank you, Miss Nene..."

"Now hurry and stand up."

That wasn't Nene. Jhin had brusquely said that as he readied his rifle in front of the girls.

Had this been a tank shell, he would have been able to cause some damage, but the most Jhin could do was stop the being with his weapon.

So what was he going to do?

"I'm going to hit my target, obviously."

A gunshot rang out.

The bullet shot through Luclezeus's chest without straying from its mark. He had hit the opening—the area that Iska had slashed through with his astral sword—the wound that had just healed.

"If he doesn't have his whole armor..."

"Did you think that would work?"

Creak.

The malformed bullet dropped to the ground. It hadn't been able to penetrate even a fraction of an inch through the giant's healed armor.

"......Tsk."

"So this is all an Imperial soldier amounts to. All a sniper amounts to. Just an ordinary Imperial sniper and bullet. You thought you could stand up to an Apostle with that?"

Luclezeus heaved a sigh. He paid Jhin's click of the tongue no heed as he turned his back on the sniper.

He faced Iska and Risya, ignoring everyone else behind him. He needed to stay on guard against the two Saint Disciples before him: the fifth seat, who could immobilize him, and the former eleventh seat, who could slice through his armor.

Only those two could be considered threats, so if he could simply defeat them, the other four would stand no chance.

...He really is thorough.

...All he wants to do is kill us.

Though he had at first aimed for Sisbell, the moment he realized he had missed, his target had shifted. He was logical to the end—frighteningly calculating, even.

"Your priorities should take precedence over all else."

He held his fist aloft.

"Risya, you erred in prioritizing the Lord over us. That mistake will cost your life."

"Quite talkative, aren't you, Luclezeus?"

"But I am different. I will make sure to take care of you and Iska first."

His fist crushed the monitors above their heads, and circles bloomed over the ceiling.

"Firmament Bloom."

It was sky-blue.

Above Iska and Risya's heads, eddies formed within the centers of the circles, and giant icicles rained down with the force of meteorites.

"...Tsk, crap!"

Risya couldn't dodge them. Instead, she made the split-second decision to make a defense using threads strung up across the ceiling to protect herself from the falling icicles at close range.

She twisted together the many wires and stopped the icicles midair.

However...

"You are quite dexterous at using that astral power."

...as though responding to Luclezeus's remark, the blue icicles tore through Risya's net.

"Even someone as extraordinary as you cannot hope to master a temporarily borrowed power."

The icicles came hailing down on Risya again. One of them

grazed Risya's nose, then burst into pieces. The tiny fragments were as sharp as razors as they gouged her.

"Ah!"

"I see. So you weren't trying to catch the icicle. You were simply trying to knock it off its course. I am impressed by your quick thinking, Risya."

"......Hearing that doesn't give me the slightest bit of joy."

A shard about the size of a knife had pierced her thigh. Risya smiled heroically in response. Her face also had cuts all over from the shower of ice fragments.

"Though you stand up to me, it will only result in more pain for you. Do you not agree, Iska, Successor of the Black Steel?"

"......Guh?!"

Iska had stopped just a few yards away from Risya. Luclezeus had said that right before he could reach her. He knew he couldn't approach the staff officer without caution after Luclezeus addressed him directly.

...He realized what I was about to do.

......Wait, no. He's just been watching me the whole time!

A chill went up Iska's spine as he thought of the unfamiliar astral power that Luclezeus had used and the peculiar caution he felt toward the Apostle.

The Apostle hadn't neglected to watch him even for a moment.

"We Apostles have reached a consensus. Successor of the Black Steel, Iska, after you defeated Kelvina, we decided you merited perpetual surveillance until your last breath."

"......Uh."

"Once we have dealt with you two Saint Disciples, then it's all over." Luclezeus declared his own victory. **"This is checkmate."**

His proclamation of their deaths rang out loudly in the room. Yet...

The giant was unaware because of his turned back. Because he had been facing Iska and Risya, he hadn't noticed the conversation occurring behind in quiet and faint whispers.

"A ruse."

A girl with red hair tied into a voluminous ponytail whispered, "I'll be in the very back."

"O-okay. I'll take the right!"

"Don't nod, boss. What are we going to do if he notices?" Jhin whispered.

He held his rifle in his right hand and Sisbell's hand in his left.

"We know not what the youth of now have in store."

The sniper let out a stifled sigh. He had recited an old idiom: The young people are not to be underestimated. How could a great person of the past know the potential of the present-day youths?

This was what Jhin had to say to the venerable generation that had held ultimate authority over the Empire.

In a hushed voice, he continued, "I don't care if they've lived for a hundred years or whatever, they're underestimating us."

3

Nebulis palace, underground.

Until minutes before, this had been a subterranean lake. The once-overflowing spring had dried and turned the place into nothing more than an underground cave of exposed rough bedrock.

And in that space...

"Come on out, Founder!" Alice was yelling so loudly her throat became dry.

She couldn't see the Founder anywhere, but she knew her voice had to be reaching outside. Her surroundings were obscured by a pitch-black curtain-like barrier.

"I know you're there! Let me out! Let me out of this sickening barrier!"

Four black spires rose from the ground. The black light emitted from the tips of those structures had spread around her like a curtain, isolating her from the surroundings she stood in.

She had been fully captured.

...She called this the Readvent Barrier?!

...I can't believe it absorbs astral energy. This is a crisis!

As for the towers that made up the barrier, they apparently absorbed all astral power, no matter how strong. It was a mage's worst nightmare, as far as prisons went.

...And I feel so strangely dizzy.

...Staying in here is putting me in danger. It's messing with my senses.

She needed to get out of there as soon as possible.

"Ice Calamity—" Alice thrust her right hand up, aiming it toward the curtain of light. "Ice Calamity—Blizzard of a Thousand Thorns!"

Hundreds of ice blades appeared, from the ground she stood upon and from midair. The daggers that Alice had created through her astral power aimed their points at the black barrier.

"Pierce!"

At her command, all blades took aim at the curtain and fired off. They were like a machine gun. The shards of ice punctured the barrier like a dense rain of bullets.

Every single one of them vanished instantaneously.

"But...?!" she cried out.

She couldn't help but feel alarmed after learning this was a prison that could seal away astral power. Could even *she* be so easily rendered powerless? Her astral powers disappeared as soon as they touched the barrier, just like snow melting in the sun.

This prison was, without a doubt, an astral mage's worst nightmare.

"...Am I really powerless to do anything?" she muttered unconsciously.

Her words echoed back to her in the isolated space.

"This is no joke!"

She chided herself for almost losing heart and falling to her knees as she fixed her posture to stand at her full height.

For Alice to have a mental breakdown—

That was likely the Founder's aim, at least.

...That's right, Alice. You already knew that. You prepared your-self for this.

...You're dealing with the Revered Founder!

She knew she would never be able to reach the ancient mage's level, even if she used all her abilities. This was the Grand Witch. And had Iska not been by her side back then, when they had been near the neutral city Ain—

...If he...

......hadn't been there, I wouldn't have won?

.........Then what about now?

............If he's not here, it's fine if I lose, is that it?

But it was the opposite.

She needed to face the Founder on her own *because* he wasn't here. If she had really prepared herself for that, she couldn't balk now.

"...So what if you're a hundred years old. So what if you're the strongest astral mage. Because you aren't! You're just a cheeky little brat!"

She clenched her fists.

She gritted her back teeth and punched the barrier before her eyes.

"You better not underestimate me!"

━━━━━━━━━

In the underground cavern, the Founder Nebulis absentmindedly stared at the black barrier.

"...In the end, all I've done is imitate the Astrals. It's far from perfect."

The barrier had a flaw. Although it might be invincible against astral mages, there was one fatal weakness. However, it wasn't particularly relevant to the princess who was currently imprisoned within the cage.

If it was applicable to anyone, that would be the Imperial swordsman who had been with Alice in the neutral city of Ain.

*   *   *

"I don't know how you've acquired them, but those cannot be used by anyone except Crossweil."

"Crossweil?! …That's the name of my master."

Crossweil Nes Lebeaxgate, the first master of the astral swords—the name was simply contrived wordplay.

His true identity was that of Crossweil Gate Nebulis, her foolish, mad younger brother.

The Founder began to speak to herself softly. Directing her words toward her brother, who had taken a different path a century ago.

"Crossweil…why did you give away your astral swords to a complete stranger? They are our secret weapon to help restore the planet. You were the one who told me that."

The two blades weren't actually swords. They were vessels in the shape of sabers, required to restore all the astral powers to the planet's core.

So why had he given them away? Just how much potential had he seen in that Imperial boy?

"Well…no good will come from thinking about it."

There was no use in discussing it. Her brother and the Imperial swordsman weren't here. There was only the princess, floundering in the astral power cage. And she could never break the prison.

"I'm sure you have nothing but dreary thoughts in your head," she said as she stared at the black barrier.

The princess was desperately trying to think of a way to escape.

Probably wondering whether there was a limit to the energy the barrier could hold. Or that it could withstand.

And the answer to both was a resounding *no*.

No matter how Alice attacked it, the black barrier would never crumble.

"Do you understand? Your attempts are futile."

Furthermore, being in the prison would distort any human's conception of time. To the princess, it likely felt as if tens of hours had passed. She should have come up with and failed at many plans by now, realizing it was useless.

That was more than enough time to break her.

"You can watch from there, girl."

The Founder turned around. She looked up, in the direction of the Empire.

"I'm going to the Empi—"

"I said I'd never let you."

Crack...

Behind the Founder Nebulis, a giant fissure had formed in the curtain.

She heard it rupture. When she realized there was something wrong, the Founder spun back around and witnessed the barrier being broken into pieces like glass.

"...Impossible."

She gulped. She thought it had been unbreakable. It couldn't be broken from the inside, at least. There shouldn't have been any astral power that a mage could use against the barrier, as it would absorb everything.

"Girl."

"...Uh...tsk... How's that? Are you scared...yet...?"

The princess didn't even have the strength to keep standing. Alice pitifully crawled along the ground on her knees, but even so, she grinned boldly as she looked up at the Founder Nebulis.

"...Who said that...I can't do anything without astral power?"

"How did you escape?"

The Founder narrowed her eyes. She glared at Alice, who clung to the wall in order to pull herself up.

"It can't be......" The Founder's eyes stopped at Alice's hands. Her skin was broken and bloodied. "So you smashed through it?"

"Yes. I gave it a good smack with my fists. I couldn't break through with my astral power, so I had to use my own body. "

She had fought her hardest.

The four spires had supported the cage. If any of them were damaged, that barrier would be destroyed. Because Alice's astral power had been rendered ineffective, she'd had no choice but to dismantle them using physical force.

"I'm not sure whether you're an absolute idiot or an absolute genius."

...*Whew*.

It was the first time the Founder Nebulis had sighed.

"If astral power won't work against it, all one needs to do is destroy it by hand. But a powerful astral mage wouldn't simply come to that conclusion. Since they would have relied on astral power since birth, after all."

"Yes, that's right...," Alice said. "I lost my way in the dark for a while."

She placed a hand on the wall and stood up. Her shoulders

heaved up and down as she said with a self-derisive smile, "But then I saw the light. I wondered just how hard the black pillars that supported the barrier could be. And after I kept punching them for a while, I thought that maybe something would come of it."

Alice had arrived at that suspicion at the eightieth hour, according to her internal clock.

Then she had continued to punch at the pillars for another ten hours.

First with her right fist, then her left. Then with her right leg, and then her left. She had even tried banging her head into them and body-slamming the pillars toward the end.

"Looks like I can do it if I set my mind to it. Those black rocks were a lot more fragile than I thought."

"That's exactly right."

"……What?"

Alice doubted her own ears.

The Founder had so easily agreed that Alice was taken aback.

"The pillars you destroyed are stones called astral crystals that exist in the planet's core. They've always been fragile. Even when I have summoned them."

"Y-you can't be serious?"

"The only ones who know the processing technique to strengthen these crystals are the Astrals, who live at the edge of the continent. You know of the perfected form already."

"What?"

"Oh? You hadn't realized?"

The Founder brushed away her pearly bangs. She looked straight up at the cavern's ceiling.

* * *

"The astral swords."

"The black crystals you broke would normally be purified to the utmost degree so they can be tempered into their perfect form. Which is what the black steel of the astral swords is."

"The astral swords?!"

The shock sent a cold shiver through Alice's whole body.

She hadn't needed to be told, nor did she need to go confirm it. Without a doubt, the black astral sword was indeed one of the swords Iska had in his possession.

"It's not my power. It's my astral swords' abilities.

"The white astral sword can release what the black one intercepts."

She remembered he had said something like that when they were in the Nelka forest. The astral swords were a black and a white blade. Whatever the black blade cut, the white could release.

…So that's what they are. If the white blade can release astral power…

…the black blade must be storing it?!

The sword wasn't actually cutting astral power.

Rather, one was storing the astral energy while the other was simply unleashing it—that was how the weapons truly worked.

The black blade would *absorb* the astral energy, which was why the astral power would temporarily disappear. To an observer, it would look as though it had been sliced through.

"Did Iska know that?"

"No idea," the Founder replied bluntly. "I doubt Crossweil told him. I'm sure he probably said that the sword can cut any astral power, and the boy believed him."

"Very likely…"

Based on how Iska acted, that was most likely the case. He had no reason to doubt and no means to suspect what the true workings of the black blade were.

"Though I couldn't care less." The dark-skinned girl turned her back on Alice. "It won't change anything."

"Huh! Stop right there!"

"I think you should be more concerned for yourself."

"……Huh?"

"What do you expect to do? You're already pale from blood loss."

Alice's vision blurred. She couldn't feel her hand resting on the wall. By the time she realized that, her slender body was already falling to the ground.

"…Wha…?"

She needed to get up. But she couldn't get her arms or legs to respond.

"Without astral power, you can't do anything. I take back what I said. I didn't think you'd break out of the astral power cage."

The barefoot girl walked away. Her pearlescent hair fluttered as she went.

"You used your whole mind and body to fight against me. I'll grant you that."

"…Wa…it…ri…ght…there…"

As her vision blurred more, she looked up frantically at the Founder. She reached toward the girl's small back. Alice gritted her teeth.

"…If you do what you want to this world…… I won't…be able to face Iska again…!"

4

"Astral energy. Don't you think it's a trifling thing?"

Luclezeus's declaration echoed throughout the large hall.

"This vessel I've put my soul into currently can only use a mere 30 percent of its abilities. This is the limit when astral power is the energy source. We Apostles desire full functionality of the vessels…or rather, the energy we seek will give us 200 percent usability."

"Sounds like a pipe dream."

"It exists, Risya. There truly exists such a power that is the stuff of dreams."

As Risya wiped the blood from her face, the giant looked down upon her and advanced, making the ground rumble with every step.

She was cornered against the wall.

"The Lord will not reach the planet's core. We will."

His fist came down with enough power to obliterate a person without leaving so much as a trace.

"Return to the planet, Risya."

"…Whoa!" Risya had leaped to the side.

She jumped off the ground with the power and nimbleness of a wild cat. Luclezeus's fist had missed by a hairbreadth.

"Ouch. I might have opened my wound…" She was holding her red and swollen shoulder.

"Risya, one more step!" Iska yelled.

She hadn't leaped far enough.

The giant's fist broke apart the floor, and when Risya's foot was caught in the fissure, she reflexively froze. Luclezeus had aimed for that from the start.

"Over here."

The mechanical soldier shot out its hand.

A cross opened on its palm, and an intense astral light began to overflow from within.

The light began to condense.

…*That light!*

…*He's going to fire the astral energy again!*

"Get down!"

As he yelled, Iska leaped to cover Risya. If Iska were to try to cut the light, he would be risking his life for that miracle. If he missed, he would be shot. He prayed as he concentrated solely on bringing down his sword.

"Nightgaze."

The flash of light stilled the air. It tried to scorch Risya. But it was cut in half by the black blade, and it disappeared.

"Oh! Isk, that was great."

"All in vain."

Luclezeus turned toward Iska. A stronger light was already glittering in his giant hands.

"…You can power it up even more?!"

"The vessel's output is infinite. It drains the energy source faster, but when it does, all I need do is obtain more."

He was attempting to shoot two beams at once.

If both were more powerful than previous ones, then…

142

"Hmm… This might be kind of bad," Risya murmured. Because she whispered quietly enough for only Iska to hear, he was sure that these were her true thoughts. "Now what to do? Say, Isk—"

The sound of a gunshot drowned out Risya's whisper.

Clank…
The bullet, which had hit Luclezeus's chest, hadn't been able to pierce his armor and simply fell to the ground.
"**…What are you playing at here?**" Luclezeus slowly turned around.
He faced Jhin, whose rifle was still faintly smoking.
"**You already tried that. My outer armor is as hard as the crystal of the Planetary Stronghold. Even a shell from a tank couldn't scratch it.**"
"I know that."
"**Don't you find it futile, then? Do you intend to give it your all, fighting with that useless rifle of yours?**"
"You're so fussy."
"**…What?**"
"So, Apostle." Jhin put down his gun. It was as though he were announcing he no longer needed it, and he remained calm and collected. "You've got a real flair for dramatics. Even a shell wouldn't scratch it? If your armor really *is* that strong, you could've cleaned us up way faster than this. You could bomb this whole hall and blow it away, or use some astral power, or something. Then we'd all die, and you'd be the only one left standing. Am I wrong?"
"____"
"But you keep choosing to use localized attacks."

He'd tried to attack Risya with his fists. Even the Nightgaze beam had been aimed straight at his targets. The flames that had reached up to the ceiling and the icicles coming down had all been concentrated on attacking a single person each time.

That was why they had continued to just barely avoid them.

...Jhin's got a point.

...Risya and I were so focused on dodging that we never picked up on it.

For the first time, Iska noticed something was off.

If Alice had been attacking them, she would have frozen the entire room. Kissing, the thorn purebred, would have buried the place with her prickles. Even the Founder Nebulis would have blown the whole place away without reservation, just as Jhin said.

But Luclezeus hadn't, impenetrable armor or not.

"This room is surrounded by the astral power barrier. So if you used an astral power that could blast us all away, not a trace of that would escape outside, am I right, Apostle?"

"_____"

"Now, is there a reason why you can't destroy this place?"

"I don't know what you're getting at."

"Then I'll tell you. It's this."

Jhin raised his gun. He brought it up like a club and hit the wall behind him, smashing the black stone pillar, which shattered.

"...The astral crystal!"

"This is one of the pillars supporting the barrier, right? There's one in each corner of the room, sprouting from the ground. Even an idiot could figure it out. But what really cinched it was your terrible performance."

"...What did you say?"

"Just now, before you shot that Nightgaze, you dramatically held up your fists. Why? That's because Risya was in one of the corners."

He had let her dodge his fist on purpose. By doing that, he had forced her to move. Because one of the stones supporting the barrier had been directly behind Risya.

He'd been afraid of the possibility of damaging it.

"You made it obvious by being so dang fussy. This barrier is super fragile near the pillars."

"**Tsk!**" Luclezeus seemed at a loss for words.

Behind him, in two corners...

"Commander, hurry over there!"

"Leave it to meee!"

Nene and Mismis, who had pulled monitors off the walls, threw the screens right at the black pillars.

The towers broke.

Luclezeus hadn't even had time to stop the two ladies as the second and third pillars were also destroyed.

That left one.

"I see. So that's why Iska and I didn't notice. We were desperately trying to dodge you, after all."

Risya readied herself. She raised her fist almost as though she were about to throw a ball.

"**W-wait, Ris—**"

"And that's four."

Clang—the pillar abruptly broke in half.

Immediately...

The black curtain covering the room disappeared like breaking clouds.

"The barrier disappeared?! That's amazing. It worked just like you said, Jhin—," Mismis started to say.

"But that changes nothing."

"……Eek?!"

When Luclezeus looked down at Commander Mismis, her face froze.

"The cage was just a bonus. We used it as a tactical measure because we want to avoid a troublesome conflict with the Lord if they catch wind of this. Nothing more."

The Lord would likely sense the battle. But the Lord was far away, in the capital. They wouldn't be able to do anything. The Apostle would succeed as long as he dealt with the witch princess.

"Now that the barrier is gone, I don't need to hold back my true power anymore. I can blow away this room using the large-scale astral power that you mentioned. You all are—"

"So there you were."

Just then, something strange happened.

The ceiling filled with dark clouds.

"…What is this?"

As Luclezeus looked dubiously above his head, the mist whirled and, slowly, a thin girl descended. Her iridescent hair fluttered. The eyes of the strongest astral mage were lit with the flames of rage.

"Did you think you could escape from me, Imperial?"

"The Grand Witch?!"

For the first time, Apostle Luclezeus looked bewildered. He

had realized it too late. Because the astral power cage had broken, the great astral energy that had collected had surged upward.

The intense amount of astral energy must have brought her here. It wasn't the Lord he should have been wary of. He couldn't have expected it would beckon the Founder.

"The disturbance we sensed near the Nebulis palace... I guessed it might be a sign of your awakening, but I didn't expect you to hunt us down all the way here, Grand Witch!"

"Disappear."

"Yes, you would do well to disappear!"

Everything happened all at once.

The Founder Nebulis raised her right hand, and Luclezeus lifted his left.

The astral power and light that they shot at each other collided.

The Nightgaze's light passed through the Founder.

However, the mage's astral power consisted of only light. It didn't create even the slightest fire or explosion, but simply illuminated Luclezeus below before fading.

"...No?!"

Luclezeus's whole body quivered in shock from what he had witnessed. He had overlooked it and forgotten which building he was in the basement of.

"I heard it from Ms. Risya," the witch princess said matter-of-factly and solemnly.

She placed a hand on her chest.

Her Illumination astral crest glittered faintly.

"This is an Imperial factory. A century ago, the factories were burned down by the Revered Founder's flames and have continued to stand abandoned. And it appears this is one of them."

"...Tsk."

"So I had an idea. In other words, the Revered Founder once was in the skies above this place!"

She had reproduced the scene. The astral power cage covering the room had finally been destroyed, and Sisbell was able to use her power again. She had only needed it to work for a moment.

After tricking Luclezeus into thinking it was the real Founder, she just needed him to direct his attention upward. That was the only moment she needed. Apostle Luclezeus had shown an opening that allowed the two Saint Disciples to attack.

"You were all amazing. Great performance."

Creak.

The threads Risya had spun warped and seized Luclezeus's limbs.

"...Risya!"

"Down here."

Iska leaped from below Luclezeus's feet. Gripping his black astral sword, he tore through the soldier's armor with the blade.

"**All of you—impertinent, all of you!**" The giant's—or rather Luclezeus's—roar made the factory grounds quake.

"**Risya, Successor of the Black Steel, witch princess, how do you not understand it's all futile?!**"

He had already proved he could rip Risya's threads. The only thing Iska's sword had been able to cut had been the armor at his breast. Even Sisbell's astral power was an illusion that was nothing to fear once the trick was discovered.

"**It's over. Everything is over. I will release all the power this**

**vessel has and scorch everything around me. You have no means
of escape…"**

"Nene, shoot!"

"Jhin, now!"

"Mismis, make sure you don't miss."

Iska, Sisbell, and Risya all shouted.

Their voices rang out beautifully together like a chorus, as
though in response to the miracle that was occurring.

Three bullets pierced Luclezeus's chest.

Iska had sliced through the armor and exposed the astral
power cage that lay within, allowing the cage imprisoning the
astral power to be hit by three bullets and break.

"………Wha…?…"

Luclezeus stopped moving. The energy source for his body had
abruptly been cut off.

"Astral power will not stay in a machine. You just told us that,
after all," Nene said, holding a handgun.

"S-so…if we just made an opening in the cage that was
restraining the astral power, it would escape on its own. You've
lost your energy source and can't move now!" Commander Mismis stuttered. "…Jhin was the one who thought up the whole plan,
though."

"Who cares about that?" Jhin said, a step behind her. He had
his favorite rifle over his shoulder.

A mysterious glitter seeped out of the giant hole in the Object's
chest and rose into the air. The astral power. The energy source
had just been set free.

"Any normal handgun and a mark thirty yards away. No Imperial soldier would miss that. As long as the target is exposed, we'd be able to hit it with our eyes closed."

"…"

"You underestimated us. Just regular old soldiers."

That had been Luclezeus's mistake.

There was no such thing as an ordinary Imperial trooper. They had seen through the mechanism behind the astral power cage, broken the pillars, and pierced the astralnomical soldier's chest with their three bullets. It hadn't been Iska or Risya alone who had accomplished those things. Each Unit 907 member had contributed to winning the battle.

"…You…"

Luclezeus swayed and lurched back as he collapsed.

"…Do you…intend to steal the planet's future…? If I, if the Apostles aren't here…then who will control that witch…?"

He muttered as if it were a curse. As though he had seen the future in his last moments. And his warning echoed: **"The world's final witch."**

Then, after using the last of his energy, the astralnomical soldier stilled.

INTERMISSION

The World's Only Knight and Witch

"*The First Princess Elletear Lou Nebulis IX.*

"*While you are still unconscious in this giant flask, I will say this. No, I suppose it isn't a confession so much as repentance. I'm disposing of you for being a failure.*"

"*You were the weakest purebred type.*

"*Your Voice astral power… Well, it's laughably weak.*"

"*But in exchange, your body held a frightening hidden potential.*

"*No one would have guessed you would still retain your ego even after fusing with* it.

"*You're dangerous. I agree with the Eight Great Apostles. If you're able to completely combine with* the thing *in the planet's core, the world will perish.*

"*So I must dispose of you.*"

Those had been…

…the last words Kelvina told her when she was still in the water cistern.

"I'm sorry, you know."

She giggled.

A small room with dim light. Elletear placed her hand on the frame of the room's window and murmured as though humming to herself while viewing the moon.

Elletear Lou Nebulis IX.

Her fluttering hair was an incredibly beautiful emerald with tinges of gold.

Her looks were as enchanting as a goddess's, and her alluring, voluptuous figure could have held any man in the world captive. If her superior beauty could be called magic, then there was no one more fittingly called a witch than the First Princess.

"I heard you loud and clear even in the tank, Kelvina. While I was unconscious, *it* heard your mutterings from within my body."

That was why she had escaped.

Because the Eight Great Apostles, who feared her power, were planning to eliminate her.

Then again...

At the moment, Elletear was the Empire's prisoner, and she was once again under the surveillance of these eight leaders of the Imperial assembly. They had even prepared this small room for her.

"..."

She looked up at the surveillance camera on the ceiling. She wondered what the Eight Great Apostles must be feeling watching her as she stared up at it. Did they feel as though they were watching a woman as beautiful as a goddess?

No.

They probably felt they were observing an unfamiliar beast—wondering what kind of monster she would become.

"Just a little longer..."

Even now, a waterfall of sweat continued to pour down Elletear's face. Constant chills and vertigo gnawed at her body. She almost felt as though she would lose consciousness. To be more precise, she felt as if her mind were being taken over. Her body was undergoing a metamorphosis.

Once her unparalleled beauty was stripped away, the most frightening monster in the world would likely make its debut. A monster that would put both the witch Vichyssoise and the fallen angel Kelvina to shame.

...*But this...*

...*This was something I wanted, that I pursued and accepted for myself.*

The *thing* that transcended astral power, the *thing* that slumbered in the planet's core. Because she had accepted its power, her body had started transmogrifying into something inhuman.

"Ugh!"

She was assaulted by a terrible urge to puke as she doubled over.

But there was nothing to vomit. She hadn't had water, much less eaten anything, for an entire week. Her stomach was empty.

...*I know, more or less...*

...*that tonight is the end of it.*

This was her last day as a human. The reason she knew was that the chills, dizziness, and even nausea felt comforting. She was overjoyed that her body was being tampered with. It had at last come.

The night she would finally fully turn into a monster.

"I'm sorry, Mother...," she said to the distant queen in the Nebulis Sovereignty.

The eldest of the three sisters rasped in agony.

"Mother...your Sovereignty...will fall. With this power... once the power inside me fully becomes mine...I won't be afraid of anything anymore... Not you, nor Alice...not even if the Revered Founder herself stands against me..."

She would surpass all astral mages and witches. She would surpass all power and authority and all astral powers.

"Even if I make the whole world my enemy, I will manipulate it into what I desire."

Clack.

She heard footsteps outside her door. When she guessed at who it could be, a small smile slowly spread across her face. It wasn't the sneer she'd had on earlier. It was her goddess smile—the expression she only showed to the person she had let into her heart.

"I don't mind. You may enter, Joheim."

The door opened. The tall, lean knight with crimson hair bowed and walked toward Elletear. The Saint Disciple of the first seat, the "Flash" Knight Joheim. He was also the Lord's guard. Most notably, he was the man who had impaled her when she protected the queen.

"The First Princess Elletear, who protected the queen, had been cut by the Saint Disciple's sword."

That very swordsman...

...now was alone together with Elletear. He knelt on one knee before her. It was almost as though...

... he was a knight protecting a princess.

"..."

157

"How rare of you to visit my room at night, Joheim." Elletear invited him closer with a gentle smile. "Thank you."

She placed a hand on the swordsman kneeling before her and caressed his head.

"My plan came this far because you are with me. If you hadn't been there when I escaped the palace, things wouldn't have turned out so well."

"..."

"Her Majesty was faintly suspicious that I was the Lou family's traitor. So I needed that act. I protected the queen, and you cut me down. That would clear me of all suspicions, would it not?"

"..."

"Oh, but please rest assured, I have already healed from the wound you gave me."

Elletear placed a hand on the thin nightgown over her chest. "You see?"

There was neither scratch nor scar.

The ghastly injury, which had seemed fatal, had healed without leaving a trace behind.

"I know you didn't want to do it, but—"

"Lady Elletear."

He was still kneeling. The knight kept his head bowed as he continued in a hushed voice, "My lady, please do not forget the pain of a humble servant asked to hurt his master."

"..."

"I will never follow an order like that again. I came here to tell you that."

"..." She blinked in surprise.

But then, a bittersweet smile formed on the emerald-haired witch's face.

"Thank you, Joheim." Her voice was tender, and not contrived. The princess's warm eyes were the greatest proof of her gratitude. "......Yes, that battle must have taken a toll on you."

In the Nebulis palace that had been assailed by the Imperial forces, Elletear had planned to be struck by a sword. The Saint Disciple had pursued the queen, and by protecting her and being cut down as a result, Elletear had been able to successfully disguise her travel to the Empire as a natural consequence of being taken away.

Only three people knew of the plot. She, Joheim, and the Hydra witch Vichyssoise.

"Now off you go. I have an important role to play soon."

"Ha! Getting wounded hurts, even if you have a body like mine. I'm sure it'll hurt even more if it's a Saint Disciple doing it."

It had all been part of Elletear's scheme.

The queen had been tricked along with the Second Princess Aliceliese. The girl hadn't been able to forgive the Imperial forces for killing her older sister—and with that single-minded thought, Alice had fought again against Iska even though she hadn't wanted to.

"Thanks to that, I've been able to defect to the Empire. I wanted to leave the Sovereignty, by any means necessary. I didn't want my mother to see her own daughter turning into a monster, after all."

"..."

"Joheim, please stand."

The Saint Disciple did as she asked. Meanwhile, Elletear sat on the window ledge. She took in the face of the man who was staring down at her.

"I think it will be tonight. In one or two hours, I'm sure I'll no longer be human. Even I don't know what grotesque form I'll take."

"Yes."

"I have no regrets. I'm doing this to achieve both our visions, after all. In order to obtain that power."

"Yes."

"But..." Elletear hesitated. She bit her lip as though she were holding back a sob that would shake her shoulders. "I'm still...just afraid of you...being frightened after seeing me......"

"..."

"You can laugh when you see me. You could even hate me from the bottom of your heart. But please...just don't be scared of me—that's all I ask!"

The room fell silent. Elletear didn't move in the slightest.

Her escort held her in a tight embrace.

"Lady Elletear."

"..."

"I am your shield. If you're the last witch in the world, then I promise I'll become the last knight in the world to protect you."

The Saint Disciple of the first seat, the "Flash" Knight Joheim.

Why had the man who normally resided in the Lord's quarters, who would normally never leave the side of the Lord for even an instant, visit an imprisoned witch deep in the night?

That was because...

...she was his true master.

In this world, they only served each other. The knight Joheim Leo Armadel only served Elletear, and Princess Elletear only had one knight—Joheim. Always.

The two had only been fighting for each other this whole time.

"I was born in the Sovereignty, and because of my weak astral power, I failed to join the astral corps. In the nation where astral power reigns supreme, there was only one person who spoke to me. Who told me that we were alike. Only you smiled and offered me a hand."

"..."

"Elletear, that's why I fight for you."

"..."

"Never doubt me. Believe in me. Use me. Order me. As long as you are you, I will continue to be your knight."

"......Oh, you. How stubborn you are."

The beautiful witch closed her eyes.

She hadn't had anything to drink in over a week. Though her skin was parched as the sands of a desert...she felt as though something would begin flowing out of her—something she couldn't stop—if she didn't close her eyes.

"Joheim."

"Yes."

"Let's destroy it together. Then let us create a true paradise on this planet alongside each other. A paradise where no one will be discriminated against, no matter how weak a human or mage they are."

"Yes."

"The Empire is in the way. They do persecute mages, after all."

"And the Sovereignty as well. The strong mages reign over the weak, and the weak astral mages look down upon those without powers."

"The Lord, too."

"And the Founder."

"And the Lou."

"And the Zoa."

"And the Hydra."

"And the Eight Great Apostles."

"And the Nebulis royal family."

"And even the astral powers."

"I will destroy them all. That is why I will become the world's last witch."

That night.

In the outskirts of the capital, an anguished scream that did not seem of this world could be heard.

And hours later...

...the delighted singing of something inhuman reverberated.

EPILOGUE

The Most Terrible Day for a Beginning

1

She opened her eyes.

Alice was lying on her bed.

"…"

"A-are you awake, Alice?!"

"Mother?"

The queen, who had been sitting next to the bed, turned to her. She was glad to see Alice able to prop herself upright. She let out a relieved sigh.

"Oh, thank goodness. When I heard from my people that you were unconscious in the underground level, I lost it. Please don't make your mother worry so."

"I was… Ouch!"

Alice winced as she held her aching head in her hand. Her brain fog was beginning to clear, and the last thing she had seen was coming back to mind.

*　　*　　*

"Founder.

"You intend to burn down the Empire, don't you?"

That was right.

The Founder Nebulis had awoken beneath the palace.

She had tried to stop it, but...

While attempting to escape from the astral power prison, she had reached her limit and exhausted all her strength.

"Your Majesty!"

She leaped from the bed.

It was fine. As long as she endured the headache and torpor, she could still move unencumbered.

"It is a grave matter! The Revered Founder has awakened from her coffin...!"

"Yes. It seems that has come to pass."

The queen was looking out Alice's window.

"A great number of our patrol officers and ministers have witnessed her. She wore a worn-out cloak and floated in the sky for some time."

"And then what happened...?"

"She vanished into thin air. But the scholars told us she doesn't have a teleportation-type astral pow—"

"I knew it!"

She gritted her teeth.

The Founder had headed to the Empire, without a doubt. She would likely head to its center and burn it down until not a piece of the capital remained.

…This is a dire situation.

…Rin is imprisoned in the Imperial capital, and Iska is there, too!

And also others from the Sovereignty. They had many spies within the Empire collecting intelligence. The Founder would likely spare them no mercy as she razed the entire place.

But she could still make it.

Before the nightmare became reality.

"Yes, all we can do is try, Alice…"

Alice clenched her fists.

She was determined. Sooner or later, she had known the time would arrive when she would need to go to the Empire herself. And the moment had simply come.

"I've decided," she said.

"Alice? What's gotten into you?"

"Your Majesty, I've put all my reservations behind me. Or rather, I can no longer tolerate waiting!"

She turned to face the queen, who had stood up.

Their gazes met, and Alice nodded deeply.

"I cannot bear to be the plaything of that arrogant little girl any longer!"

"Little girl?"

"I mean to say the Revered Founder."

"Huh?! A-Alice, what has gotten into you? How could you call the Revered Founder that…?"

"But it's true. She's caused a great amount of trouble for us!"

Alice released all her pent-up frustrations.

Her voice resounded throughout the room as she declared, "I will go to the Empire. I will stop the Founder! And then I will save Rin!"

2

Imperial capital.

Divided into three sectors, this city was known to be the most densely populated in the world.

Sector One was where the government and research facilities were gathered. Here, the assembly would convene and use its full authority to decide all political matters of the Empire.

Sector Two was the residential area, where 70 percent of the Imperial capital's populace lived. Next door was the world-leading business district that tourists all over the world visited.

Then there was Sector Three, the base of operations for military affairs. It was the permanent residence of the Imperial forces and had numerous training facilities.

"So we've finally made it to the capital..."

In front of a large vacant area of Sector Two, Sisbell looked up at the sky after getting out of the car. It was already the middle of the night. The sun had set beyond the horizon, and the faint gloom of the sky expanded.

Though it was so late, the Imperial capital's sky wasn't pitch-black, but rather still bright.

"The night sky... It makes me feel uneasy." Sisbell seemed somewhat exasperated as she sighed. "The Second Sector, was it? The light from the buildings of the business district is so bright that I can't even see the stars. This would be unthinkable in the Sovereignty."

"Shh, they'll overhear us, Miss Sisbell," Commander Mismis whispered in a panic.

The capital was the most strictly guarded city in the world. The entire place was equipped with surveillance cameras and astral energy sensors.

"Hey, Jhin, we've finally made it home, haven't we?"

"Sure have. Home is home, whether it's been a while or not."

"But I'm not sure I'm happy about it...," Nene said. "I think I'm more nervous."

"We've got a huge job to do, that's for sure."

Jhin and Nene were both looking up ahead at the checkpoint.

It was stationed at the Sector Three entrance. But the operation base and maneuvering grounds, the military site, and many other locations that lay there were not their goal.

The Castle Tower Seat.

They were headed to the building where Lord Yunmelngen awaited—the windowless structure where Rin was imprisoned as well.

"An audience with the Lord. I don't even want to think about what's waiting for us. Iska, you've been in the tower before, right?"

"Just once..." Iska nodded demurely beside Jhin.

It had been back when he had successfully risen to the position of Saint Disciple. However, when he had been granted the audience, the Lord's body double had actually appeared before Iska.

This time it would be different.

The true Lord Yunmelngen would be waiting there.

Moreover, there were also those who did not want nor would allow them to make contact with the Lord.

...Risya said that Luclezeus's cyberbrain disappeared.

...Since we defeated him, they're going to come after us.

They had made the Eight Great Apostles their enemies.

They couldn't let their guard down, even in the capital. There was the danger they would eventually be attacked by assassins under the patronage of these eight leaders of the Imperial assembly.

"All riiight! Sorry for the wait, everyone!"

Risya, who had been in the car, disembarked after them.

Her face was covered in bandages, as was her thigh.

Those were, needless to say, a result of their fight with one of the Eight Great Apostles. Despite that, she showed no sign of pain, and her tone was aloof as ever.

"We've gotten in touch with Their Excellency. We need to head over to the tower right away to make sure we don't keep them waiting. In an hour, we'll have an audience with the Lord."

"Um... If I could ask a question?"

"What is it, Isk?"

"So about the Eight Great Apostles..."

"Hm? Oh, I reported about that, too, of course. That they're going to rebel against the Lord."

They were in a vacant lot in the capital.

Though they couldn't tell whether anyone was listening, Risya didn't seem to care in the slightest.

"But the Lord was expecting that. The important thing isn't my report—it's for the Lord to see it."

"Using Sisbell's astral power?"

"That's right. That's why we came all the way here. So let's head out."

Risya pointed at the checkpoint and started walking toward it, feeling exultant.

Iska followed her, but just as he did...

"......Hm?"

He felt something.

A faint, truly faint sense of nostalgia.

Was it the footsteps? The smell?

Though he didn't understand what it was, Iska turned around as though attracted to it.

And he saw an unbelievable sight.

"......It can't be..."

"Can't be what, my idiot disciple?"

"...Why are you here...Master?"

"Are you really that surprised I returned to the capital?"

That listless tone.

And that head-to-toe black outfit that hadn't changed since all those years ago.

Iska's teacher, Crossweil Nes Lebeaxgate, stood there before him.

He still wore a long coat about his figure, so slim it didn't have a single bit of excess body fat.

The former Saint Disciple of the first seat. The former master of the astral swords. And the man who had been Iska and Jhin's teacher.

It had happened years ago. He had given Iska his own astral swords and Jhin a sniper rifle, then left the capital without a trace.

Iska couldn't believe they had reunited at a time and place like this.

"Huh, it's Master Cross?!"

"Wait...Master Cross? You mean that's your teacher, Iska and Jhin?!"

Nene and Commander Mismis widened their eyes. Next to them, Sisbell only tilted her head to the side quizzically without an idea of what was happening.

"Wh-what's going on here?! Why are you all so worked up…? Jhin? Who in the world is this man supposed to be?"

"He taught Iska and me."

"……Come again?"

"I'm just as surprised as you are. I don't understand what's going on. It's all too sudden."

There was a rare, strained smile on Jhin's face as he answered. For the sharpshooter, whose job was to anticipate anything, this unforeseen arrival was likely distressing.

"Hey, Master, what even brought you here?"

"What?"

"I find it hard to believe we'd just run into you in a place like this now of all times. So I can only assume you were waiting for us. Or is this your doing, Ms. Staff Officer?"

"Who, me?"

When Jhin glared at her, Risya shrugged.

"I'd like to know that, too. It's nice to meet you, former first seat Crossweil. I have heard much about you from the Lord."

"About that."

Iska's master wasn't looking at Risya, but instead straight at Iska.

"If you're going to see Yunmelngen, you ought to hurry."

Crossweil didn't say "the Lord" but used Yunmelngen's actual name—the name of the highest authority within the Empire.

"That's all I'm here for."

"What?! Wait...Master?!"

Iska wasn't able to stop him in time. Before any of them knew it, the former teacher had turned his back on them and started walking toward the business district.

"What is wrong with him?! I've got a ton of things I want to ask him—"

"I'm busy."

"But wait!"

"I've got to go console the most ferocious threat in the world before she throws a tantrum. She's probably just about to reach the Imperial border."

".......?"

"Ask Yunmelngen about the rest. He might not be pretty to look at, but he's not a scoundrel at the very least."

Iska couldn't understand it.

After they'd finally reunited all these years later, what was his master trying to tell him? Crossweil pretended he had not seen Iska's bewildered face.

The former owner of the astral swords disappeared into the crowd.

3

At around the same time...

The Castle Tower Seat.

Deep inside the windowless, gigantic structure.

*   *   *

"The planet has a memory of all phenomena that occur on its surface."

It was like a song. Like a poem being recited. The silver-furred beastperson—Lord Yunmelngen—looked up at the vermilion ceiling and hummed.

"I'm looking forward to it. My blood is racing. Hurry, witch of Illumination."

"Call Lady Sisbell by her name," said someone who sounded rather peeved.

Behind the standing Lord, Rin pouted where she sat on the tatami.

"So we'll see Lady Sisbell soon, then? I'll have you know that you'd better not call her a witch to her face."

"Yes, yes."

"Do you really understand?"

"*I* won't do that."

"Hm?" Rin raised an eyebrow.

The beast's slightly sarcastic words implied that the *Lord* wouldn't call her a witch, but someone else would.

"You little—"

"I have something to say to you, too. You should get ready. The Third Princess Sisbell is coming. And we'll finally see who was behind everything."

Lord Yunmelngen was still staring at the ceiling.

"The tragedy that occurred a century ago."

"What did you say?"

"The birth of the Founder Nebulis. Of me. Of the Black Steel Gladiator, Crossweil. Also the reason why the astral swords were made. And for what slumbers at the planet's core."

Namely...

For the first time, Rin saw the rage in their expression as they spoke.

"We will shortly witness the worst day on this planet."

Lord Yunmelngen sought the truth.

The Founder Nebulis had vowed to have her revenge. Her younger brother was rushing to stop her.

And the Eight Great Apostles were laying and pushing ahead with their schemes.

Rin, Risya, Unit 907. The Successor of the Black Steel Iska and the second princess, Alice, who had decided to head to the Empire. Then the royal families of the Zoa and Hydra, who had set out for the Empire with other motives.

And then...

...the witch who disparaged them all.

Only seventeen hours remained until all the forces on the planet would collide.

Afterword

If you're the last witch in the world, I'll become the last knight in the world.

Thank you for picking up the tenth volume of *Our Last Crusade or the Rise of a New World*!

This volume's theme was "buildup."

All the characters in this story are gathering in the Empire. This is the final countdown.

In the Sovereignty, the Zoa and Hydra are honing their claws.

In the Empire, powerful people are beginning to clash and fight.

In the next volume, the events that occurred a century ago in the Empire will finally be revealed. The story of the Founder, the Lord, and Iska's teacher is starting!

Besides that...

Now, about the opening statement of this afterword. It is a line from one of the characters, but it was also the temporary title I used before deciding on *Last Crusade*.

Then the story began to take shape...

Once the current title of *Last Crusade* was settled on, I had another couple take the mantle for the line from Iska and Alice. I would be so happy if you would watch how this change develops in the future of the story.

...Well, then! Without further delay, I have information about a fan favorite—the anime.

The anime should be streaming by the time this volume is in bookstores, but since I have the opportunity, I'd like to announce it again.

The anime *Our Last Crusade or the Rise of a New World* is airing!

▼ *Last Crusade* the TV Anime is Airing
① The Broadcasters
- AT-X starting 11:30 PM on Wednesdays (with early and repeat broadcasts)
- ABC TV 2:14 AM Wednesdays
- Tokyo MX1 1:35 AM Wednesdays
- TV Aichi 2:35 AM Wednesdays
- BS11 1:00 AM Fridays

② Streaming
- dAnimeStore midnight Wednesdays (prior to TV broadcast, fastest independent broadcaster)

It'll be on other anime streaming sites as well.

※ Please check the *Last Crusade* official anime site for details.

* * *

▼ *Last Crusade* Online Radio Broadcast

In addition to the anime, there will also be an online radio broadcast!

Based on the lineup, it's going to be great. None other than Yusuke Kobayashi, who voices Iska, and Sora Amamiya, who voices Alice, will be hosting the radio show.

The broadcast will be called *Yusuke Kobayashi and Sora Amamiya Last Crusade RADIO.*

They plan on holding it every other week on Tuesdays starting October 6.

I'm looking forward to finding out what they'll say about *Last Crusade.* In addition to Kobayashi and Amamiya, there may be other guests from the *Last Crusade* anime.

They are currently gathering fan letters, so if you send some in, they might use them!

I hope you enjoy the online radio broadcast along with the anime!

▼ Opening and Ending

· OP "Against"

The opening theme, sung by Kaori Ishihara, will be on sale on November 4.

Personally, I like how the first scene shown in the opening is from the first episode. I hope you'll watch the show and enjoy it! I'd be so happy if you did!

· ED "Ice Birdcage" & insert song "Sora Étranger"

Aliceliese's (VA: Sora Amamiya) ending and insert song will be on sale on November 11.

The insert song is really beautiful, so I hope you're looking forward to hearing it when it's used in the anime!

I've already ordered it online!

The OP and ED are both perfect, so I hope that you'll listen to them!

▼ Other Anime News

Aliceliese is being made into a figurine.

I had the opportunity to see the 3D model, and every detail of her dress is gorgeous. They even got every strand of her hair perfect.

I want you to see the finished version soon!

And I'll tell you about the other merchandise on my Twitter!

...Well then.

There were many things to report about the anime, and I'll be most happy if you watch the first episode.

I hope you'll support the anime versions of Iska and Alice as well!

There's one other piece of news I have that's not related to *Last Crusade*.

Why Does No One Remember My World?, which I've been writing alongside *Last Crusade* for MF Bunko J, has reached a good stopping point.

And so...

I'd like to announce a new story!

▼ *God's Games We Play*

The gods challenge humanity, and humanity must win ten games against these capricious deities. But in the history of mankind, no one has yet to clear all ten and beat them at their own game, the games of the gods.

This is the story of a boy who represents all of humanity in a battle of intellect against these supreme beings.

It's serialized on the novel website Kakuyomu!

Among the series I have written, this was by far the most challenging for me, so I asked for permission to deliver it to you early through online installments.

Even though it only just started serialization, it's a huge hit!

The series setting is a somewhat unusual world with a combination of intellectual battles and high fantasy.

I hope you'll casually read it during lunch breaks or during your commute to work or school. I'll work hard on this alongside *Last Crusade*, so I hope you'll have high expectations for it!

Well, then...

Continuing on, I have an announcement about the *Last Crusade* novels.

▼ *The Last Crusade Secret File Volume 2* Short Stories
They're slated for release on December 19, 2020.

A tale of the swordsman Iska and the witch princess Alice.

The second volume will focus on what happens behind the scenes in the two's lives.

Fortuitously, the two stories in the first volume were so well received that I'm going to work hard on the new ones for the second volume.

It will be published in December while the anime is airing, so I hope you're looking forward to it!

And so the afterword has come to an end.

Many people helped me with this volume, as always.

To the illustrator, Ao Nekonabe: Thank you so much for the beautiful cover illustration of Alice! The anime has already started to broadcast. I'm really looking forward to the moment when I'll see the Iska and Alice you drew being animated. I'm writing the afterword in September, so I can't wait for October!

To my editors O and S, it was so reassuring that both of you were doing everything you could to support me through the novels of *Last Crusade* to the anime. I hope you'll continue to help me drum up even more support for *Last Crusade*!

Well, then...

The afterword is almost over now, too.

I'll see you in December 2020 for *Last Crusade*'s second volume of short stories.

And *Last Crusade*'s eleventh volume in spring of 2021.

And I hope we'll meet in *Last Crusade*'s anime!

In September, when summer has just ended,

Kei Sazane

O planet, show me your past. Sisbell's power illuminates the events of a century ago...

These are the struggles and battles of the man who will become Iska's teacher. The Nebulis siblings, a young Crossweil and his twin sisters, having arrived at the Imperial capital, encounter a child who claims to be the Lord. At the same time, deep beneath the capital, a plot is brewing that will shake the whole world.

The eleventh act, a dance between the most powerful swordsman and the supreme witch. Do not forget, Iska. These swords are our only hope to restore the planet.

OurLast CRUSADE OR THE RISE OF A NewWorld

VOLUME 11

Anticipated for early 2023!

HAVE YOU BEEN TURNED ON TO LIGHT NOVELS YET?

86—EIGHTY-SIX, VOL. 1-11

In truth, there is no such thing as a bloodless war. Beyond the fortified walls protecting the eighty-five Republic Sectors lies the "nonexistent" Eighty-Sixth Sector. The young men and women of this forsaken land are branded the Eighty-Six and, stripped of their humanity, pilot "unmanned" weapons into battle...

Manga adaptation available now!

WOLF & PARCHMENT, VOL. 1-6

The young man Col dreams of one day joining the holy clergy and departs on a journey from the bathhouse, Spice and Wolf. Winfiel Kingdom's prince has invited him to help correct the sins of the Church. But as his travels begin, Col discovers in his luggage a young girl with a wolf's ears and tail named Myuri who stowed away for the ride!

Manga adaptation available now!

SOLO LEVELING, VOL. 1-5

E-rank hunter Jinwoo Sung has no money, no talent, and no prospects to speak of—and apparently, no luck, either! When he enters a hidden double dungeon one fateful day, he's abandoned by his party and left to die at the hands of some of the most horrific monsters he's ever encountered.

Comic adaptation available now!